LITTLE AMERICA

THE TERRANCE YOUNG STORY

Cover designed by Hiram Williams and Joseph Johnson Jr.
Cover Designer Hiram Williams

This book is a work of fiction. Names, characters, places, and incidents either are products of the author's imagination or are used fictitiously. Any resemblance to actual persons, living or dead, events, or locales is entirely coincidental.

Joseph Johnson Jr.

Printed in the United States of America

First Printing: 2020
Camp5 Entertainment

ISBN-13 978-0-578-63209-4

I would like to thank everyone that was a part of this journey, because of you I was able to accomplish my goal of writing my own book... Words can never explain how thankful I am for the love, motivation and the push given to me...

First, I would like to thank the love of my life, Demitria Peterson, for being by my side and putting up with all of my craziness...

Next, I would like to thank La Toya Jones, for stepping in and helping me when I needed you the most. I thank you sis, and I don't care what you say, you are not paying for a copy of my book!!

I also must give a special shout out to my family, Adrian Braswell!! I did it cousin, you have always believed in me. Iron sharpen Iron...

Last but most important to my kids, remember you don't always have to lead the race, you just have to finish strong... I love all of y'all to the moon and back!

To all the readers I hope you enjoy this book as much as I enjoyed writing it.

All my motivation comes from within, the negative energy just fuels the motivation...

Sincerely,

Joseph Johnson Jr

Chapter 1

Early Sunday morning, ham, eggs, grits, and pancakes were cooking at the Smith's residence, but Terrance couldn't eat. Still high from the night before, he hadn't gotten any rest in the last 48hrs. His seven-year-old twins, nephew Jaylin and niece Lailah, were all starting to move around the house. The sky was clear and the sun was bright. Terrance was still high, drunk, and exhausted from a hell of a weekend. There would definitely be no church for him today. In all honesty, he had not been to church since family day three years ago, so missing church was nothing new to him or granny...

Grandma Joanne yelled from upstairs, "Terrance are you going to church with me this morning baby?"

"Not today granny!" He headed to the bathroom for a well-needed shower.

When Terrance stepped out of the shower, Tee saw his phone had six missed calls and two voicemails from Kay.

He shook his head, wishing now he hadn't unblocked her number. Before he could listen to her voicemails, the phone rang again.

"Hello?"

"Terrance. What the fuck? You've been out all-night doing God knows what, with God knows who, not answering your phone. Why am I home alone waiting on your ass to get here?"

"Baby, I—It' s

"What?" shouted Kay. "Save your lame-ass excuses! I am sick of this and you! And how is it Pistol Pete can make it here, but you can't?"

Terrence sighed. "Because he is your security and he lives in the guest house"

"Whatever Terrance! Where are you now?"

"I am at Grandma Joanne's house about to get some rest. I knew you were not going to let me sleep if I came home"

"Whatever nigga bye!"

The phone went dead in his ear. Terrance let Kay talk to him like that, because he knew that he was wrong for blocking her number and staying out all night. Terrance thought to himself that it would be better to address her slick ass mouth after he had got himself some efficient rest, right now Terrance didn't have the energy to fight with her.

Kay was a beautiful caramel princess with no problems of turning heads wherever she went. Her body was banging and she had a head full of long pretty jet-black hair. She was raised in a middle-class family and her parents had been married her whole life—what the fellas from the wrong side of the tracks liked to call raised right. Smart, independent, pretty, and trustworthy, with an attitude to go along with the total package.

Terrance smiled as he laid in bed thinking about his future wife, how she was probably laying in bed watching *Scandal* with just his shirt on. Yes, Kay may have been a little crazy and jealous at times, but Terrance knew Kay loved him unconditionally, that was never something that he had to second guess.

"Terrance! Terrance!" Granny's voice finally broke him out of his deep meditation, that was just a few moments from being perverted.

"I am on my way to church baby. There's some food in the microwave if you want to eat something."

"Okay granny. Make sure you say a prayer for me!"

"I always do!" He heard her close the front door behind her and the lock slide in place.

Bang, Bang, bang! Shots rang out, women screamed, and the crowd scattered in every which way. In the midst of the gun-smoke was the Down 4 Myne Crew. Their leader was a young fly fella called Lucky Lefty. Back in high school, he played basketball, football, baseball, sold dope, and had all the women. He was what the old heads called a natural. For the most part he was a level-headed fella, but his right-hand man, "Quick Money," was a loose cannon always looking for action or trouble. He was only twenty-five and had already been to prison twice on short bids.

Tracy yelled, "Get your dumb asses in the car! Don't you see all these police out here? Have you lost your mind?" Quick Money and the crew jumped in and they sped off into the night.

When they arrived at the spot, "Quick Money" was still hype filled with adrenaline from the incident that just happened at the club.

Lucky Lefty was sitting in a black recliner smoking a cigar, like nothing had happened. He knew "Quick Money" was a loose cannon, but he always knew no one would ever be as loyal to him as Quick was. One time in the 4th grade Lucky Lefty was being bullied by a 5th grader that was much bigger than them. "Quick Money" beat the kid so badly with a baseball bat that they expelled him from school for the next two years.

"Lucky, did you see Terrance at the table across from us with them entertainers and athlete niggas? What do you think he was trying to do?" asked Fox.

Lucky paused for a second and gave Fox a cold stare then replied, whatever he trying to do we cool, as long as he stays the fuck out of *my way*!" Lucky Lefty and Terrance were once good friends that became fierce enemies.

Terrence finally woke up at three pm. Tee was ready to eat a whole chicken; and eight sides Tee was so hungry. The first person he called was Kay.

"Hello?"

"What's up with my love?"

"Look, the dead have arisen," said Kay.

"Come on, bae, why do you gotta act like that?"

"Oh so now I am your bae? Last night I couldn't get your sorry ass to answer your phone!"

"Okay enough with the insults. Meet me at Island Choice restaurant. Let's sit down and grab a bite to eat," said Terrance.

"Okay I am at my parents' house. I have to stop by the store and then I will meet you," Kay replied.

"Cool!" responded Terrance.

Terrance jumped up and washed his face, brushed his teeth, and got dressed. He was 6'1'' tall and 185 lbs. Not light skin but not dark either, brown eyes, with smooth soft skin. You could see why the ladies loved him. They called him pretty-boy Terrance in high school.

Pulling out of Grandma Joanne's yard, the cellphone rang and the screen said it was Pistol Pete.

"What's up my brother from another mother?" said Pistol Pete.

"On my way to meet your crazy sister to grab something to eat."

"Boy, that's another story. She was banging on the guest house door like the police at six in the morning. She came in on me and my little shorty, knocking my hustle talking about your ass all morning. The Lil chick I had with me fell asleep on me because she was talking about you for so long."

"Go handle that my G. We'll meet at the honeycomb hideout later "

"Alright then," said Terrance.

*   *   *

Kay pulled up to the Publix. She needed to grab a few items for the house. Kay slammed on her breaks. "What the fuck?"

Some fool in a white Tahoe damn near ran into her brand-new Range Rover cutting across the front row of the parking lot by the grocery entrance of the store. When she jumped out of the car about to start cursing, she saw it was Lucky Lefty.

"Negro you almost ran into my truck!"

He laughed. "Chill K. I am not going to run into your precious truck. If I did, I can afford to pay for it, all cash! Lucky had a smirk on his face. How have you been?"

"Good. Just going to work and home is all a chick has time for these days." She glanced at the tall guy Lucky was with. She didn't recognize him.

"Are you still with ole boy?" Lucky asked, trying not to sound like he was hating.

"Who Terrance? Yes, that's still my baby."

"Damn I couldn't tell how that nigga had all them bitches in his section last night," said the tall one.

"Come on Quick Money, that was a low blow!" Lucky Lefty said.

Kay gave Quick a hard stare and told Lucky bye as she went into the store.

Damn Quick Money what's up with that, asked Lucky Lefty? Fuck that nigga, and his bitch. We should have kidnapped the bitch anyways Quick Money said.... Lucky shook his head at Quick as they drove off...

Chapter 3

Terrance pulled into Islands Choice parking lot and hopped out of his Ford Raptor, with the ATV's sitting on the trailer hooked up to the truck. Every Sunday Terrance and his crew rode their four wheelers and dirt bikes around the neighborhood. Normally in the summertime, they would often put their jet skis in the lake and barbecue on Saturdays.

Today was Sunday and usually that meant Hush Mouth City for chunky Sunday's. Islands Choice was a Caribbean restaurant with the finest Jamaican food in the area. It was so good that the European customers ate there just as much as the minority customers.

As expected, Kay's slow ass was not there yet, but Terrance already knew what she wanted so he ordered plates for them. Sitting down waiting on the food and Kay, he heard a familiar voice. It was the biggest kingpin in the city, Jamaican Fresh. He had given Terrance some valuable lessons back in the day when Terrance and his crew were sticking up everything that moved. The thought never crossed his mind to rob Jamaican Fresh; he had too much respect for the old head and respect was the only thing that would keep you alive in these crazy streets...

"Where is your beautiful woman, my youth?" asked Jamaican Fresh. "It's time to put a ring on it, King."

Terrance laughed, but he knew Fresh was serious. Fresh was a real Raster-faring deep in religious belief. Saved by the bell, Kay walked in, looking excited to see Fresh. They hugged and kissed.

"Where is my Mrs. Pat?" Kay asked.

"She is home with the grandkids; I will tell her that you asked about her," said Fresh. As Fresh walked out the door he pointed and winked at Terrance.

Kay sat down at the table, her smile instantly turning angry. "So, who are these bitches you had all in your section stunting last night big baller? You know how you like to get all in the club and show your ass, I am not going through this with you, and these thirsty females anymore, Terrance".

"What the fuck are you talking about Kay? I was out with some clients last night and shit got a little wild. I was cool. I don't have time for the thirst traps."

"Uh huh, whatever. Don't let me find out anything different. So how is business going anyways?"

"It's going, I mean of course it's not the dope game or the major heist takedowns anymore, but it's putting food on the table and life is much safer and calm," said Terrance.

"So how is everything going at your office? Did you sell any houses this week?"

"As a matter of fact, I sold three!"

She started singing! "I am hustler homie you better ask about me!"

Terrence shook his head. He couldn't help but think about how much he loved and adored this woman.

"Guess who I bumped into today?" asked Kayla. "Or should I say almost bumped into me?"

"Who?"

"Kenny Thomas."

"Who? Lucky Lefty?" Screamed Terrance.

"Yes, he had some thug with him named Quick Money. Who in the hell would name themselves Quick Money anyways?" Kay wondered out loud.

"What happened Kay? What that nigga had to say?"

"Nothing much. He just asked how I was doing and if we were still together?"

"That isn't none of his damn business, dude violating for real."

"It's okay baby, I already handled it; you have a rider on your side. Enjoy your food. You are going to need all of your strength when we get home," said Kay with a sexy look on her face.

Terrance and Kay pulled up to their house in the hammocks. The house was a two-story, six-bedroom house with a four-car garage, guest house, and a pool. A modern-day mini mansion, with all the toys and accessories to go with it. Kay pulled up in the garage and went upstairs. Terrance went into the back yard to check on his two babies. He hadn't seen them since Friday. Princess and King were his two all-white Dogo Argentinas. They were only ten months old, but they were already as big as a full-grown Rottweiler.

"Hey babies," said Terrance. "Daddy missed yawl." You could tell they were happy to see him also the way that they were jumping up and down wagging their tails. The Princess was more aggressive than the King, she needed all the attention all the time. "Women."

Terrance walked in the house, washed his hands, and grabbed a bottle of water out of the refrigerator. Leaning on the counter, he looked around to appreciate the things God was blessing him and Kay with; it was a really humbling sight to see. Who would have thought a kid from the projects would have come this far and done so well for himself. There was still much more to do, still goals to be accomplished.

His phone started to vibrate. It was his assistant, Lisa, texting about a business meeting on Monday. Confirming to see if the meeting was still a go. *Yes, the meeting is still a go Lisa,* typed Terrance. *Let's do it at ten-thirty am tomorrow, have a great day.*

"Terrance! Come here, hurry!" Kay screamed.

Terrance ran up the staircase as fast as he could; he was sure that he had missed a few steps. "What's wrong Kay?" She was sitting on the California King bed, crying, holding something in her hand. Terrance grabbed her hand only to see a white stick-shaped object.

Kay looked up still crying, but now Terrance could see the joy in her tears. "Baby, we are pregnant!" Terrance fell back lifeless on the bed...

Chapter 4

THE DOWN 4 MYNE CREW

The block was filled with people in Highway Park. It was just another Sunday in Lake Placid.

The Down 4 Myne Crew was posted up at the four-way stop, right by the Liquor store playing music sitting on their cars. All the girls wanted a piece of Lucky Lefty, but they knew better, his long-time girlfriend Tracy was crazy as hell. She once cut a chick's face and body up so badly with a razor that the State Attorney wanted to charge her with attempted murder. Tracy got off because she was only a minor and her parents had a little bit of money. She only caught five years of felony probation, a slap on the wrist compared to the damage she did to the other girl's face.

Lucky was sitting in his white Tahoe smoking a cigar and drinking D'usse' Cognac, talking to Fox and Slim about a business deal that went bad on Wednesday.

Fox said, "Man, Lucky, I felt like something was wrong the way dude was calling me saying that he really needed it now. Kim saved me bro. She told me to go, but don't take anything, just ride and check the scene. So that's exactly what I did."

Lucky Lefty asked him, "Well whose resources did this come from?"

Slim was sitting there quiet as a church mouse.

Fox got irritated and screamed, "Speak up nigga! This was your motherfucking source. I never liked this nigga anyways Lucky!"

Lucky put up his hand as if to say chill! Fox immediately calmed down. Slim started stuttering, "Luc, Luc, Luc, Lucky I didn't know, I swear. I thought dude was legit... "

Fox couldn't help himself. "Fuck nigga you don't get paid to think. You get paid to know..."

Slim was from Belle Glade. He got down with the crew, because he did time upstate with Spider, Lucky Lefty's older brother. Spider got locked up back in the day when Lucky was 16, caught life plus 40. Lucky Lefty told Slim everything was cool, just next time to do his research more thoroughly.

Quick Money was leaning on his four-door drop-top 1976 Chevy Impala, smoking a blunt talking shit as usual. The crew was laughing at every joke as if this nigga was Kevin Hart or something. Pistol Pete passed by banging Tyrese's "I want to go there" album, out of his CLS 550. His wife, Tonya, was with him.

Tonya was Terrance's older sister; she and Pete had two kids together. They had been separated for like a year now. They still remained good friends. Tonya got tired of all the games and told Pete until he was ready to be a fully committed husband he needed to leave. Sunday was the day that they came together to show the kids some family structure. Tonya saw the way the dudes at the four-way stop were looking in the car at them. She immediately warned Pistol Pete about it, but he was already on point and hit Highway 27 headed back to Avon Park.

"Yeah T, that's the fools that we used to do business with. They are jealous of me and Terrance."

"For what?"

"I don't know. No matter what you do niggas are going to hate."

"Everybody wants your spot when you are on top," said Tonya. "Just take me and my kids to the water park so we don't have to worry about all the foolishness and drama."

Pete laughed and said, "I can dig it. Let's go!"

*   *   *

Later on,... Slim pulled up to an abandoned warehouse and jumped out of the car still thinking about how close he was early to being figured out. How did the DEA agents slip up and get made by Fox? This motherfucker was the dumbest nigga in the crew. When Slim entered the warehouse, Detective Jones said, "What's up Slim? We missed your boy Fox yesterday. He never showed up, but we will get him next time."

"Next time!" Slim yelled. "He did show up and he made some of your team. They questioned me about this today. Remember it's my life on the line when yawl fuck up and make mistakes, not yours," said Slim.

Detective Smith, the lead detective on the Down 4 Myne Crew case, told Slim to calm down and apologized for his agents' screw up. They were too close to Lucky Lefty and couldn't afford to alert him of it too soon...

*   *   *

Lucky pulled up into Las Palmas, some luxury townhouses on the outskirts of Avon Park, to meet with Jackie. Jackie was a retired FBI agent; she was shot in the line of duty during an undercover operation infiltrating a Mexican Cartel. By the grace of God, she got out with her life. Now she was behind the desk pushing papers for the local sheriff's office.

"What brought you here today handsome?" she asked Kenny.

"I need you to check out some information for me. Plus... I wanted to see your fine ass," said Lucky Lefty. Jackie was Puerto Rican and black and in her early thirties. She reminded Kenny of Evelyn Lozada, banging face and body!

Chapter 5

Kenny started kissing on Jackie's neck and rubbing on her breast, pressing his hard manhood against her soft ass. She had on a black laced sundress with no panties, as Lucky put his hand on her wet vagina, she started to moan and grind on his manhood. Jackie turned around and pushed Lucky away to give herself some room to go on her knees and put all of his manhood into her mouth. Lucky grabbed Jackie by her hair and started mouth fucking her as she played with her own vagina clit. Lucky couldn't take it anymore, after laying Jackie on her back and eating her vagina, he pushed his manhood inside of her. She took a deep breath gasping for air, then she wrapped her legs around Lucky and started throwing herself on him from the bottom. She was so good that Lucky could never last long the first round with Jackie, after five minutes of being in her wet walls he was shooting waterfalls.

After two intense rounds of great sex and a shower, Jackie cooked lemon chicken, black beans, and rice with Coronas and lime to wash it down.

"So, Kenny besides this good Puerto Rican pussy, what's the information you need that's bothering you?" asked Jackie.

"The other day one of my guys almost ran into a trap with some Narc Boys. I just need to know how much they know, and if I have a mole in my crew," said Lucky.

"Kenny, you know you can't do this shit forever right? I am not going to be able to save you every time. What happened to Terrance and you? I really liked him. Why don't you go straight like he did? Because you can't dodge the authorities forever. I don't want to lose you baby!"

"Fuck Terrance and the authorities. Just find out the fucking information and call me when you get it!" Lucky grabbed his shit and slammed the door on his way out.

*   *   *

Terrance and Kay were laying in the bed debating on baby names betting on the gender of the baby. Kay wanted a baby boy and Terrance wanted a baby girl so that he could spoil her to death. Looking into Kay's eyes, Terrance started remembering the first time he had ever seen her walking down the bread aisle in Walmart with her mom when they were only fifteen. It was at that moment that he knew that he was truly in love with this woman. She had been by his side through all the lies, cheating, and hustling. He knew he had to marry her; she was the perfect woman for him. It's like Kay knew what Terrance was thinking, like she could read his mind. She smiled and kissed his lips softly as if to say I love you more.

Kay rolled Terrance over on his back and mounted his body, rubbing her hands on his chest she started to kiss Tee. Terrance was already hard as hard can be. He could feel Kay's wet vagina making smacking sounds as she grinds on him through the basketball shorts, he was wearing.

Kay asked Terrance in a soft tone, "Do you want this pussy?"

He responded "Yes!"

"Do you need this pussy?"

"Yes!"

"Well baby daddy let me feel you get this pussy!"

Before she could say anything, else Terrance was already in her, squeezing her ass and pulling her closer. They made love for the next 20 minutes straight. Kay was screaming, "I am about to cum baby please cum with me!"

Terrance said, "Ok let's do it!" They both were shaking uncontrollably when it was over! After laying there for a few minutes Terrance broke the silence by saying, "Damn that pregnant pussy was good."

Kay started laughing and said, "Boy shut up and let's go take a shower with your crazy self."

The phone beeped. It was Pistol Pete.

"Hello."

Terrance answered, "What's up Pistol?"

Pete started laughing. "Damn boy you went back to sleep?"

"Hell yeah," Tee replied. "That good food and your sister put me back out like a light bulb."

"Too much information Tee, too much damn information," Pistol Pete replied while laughing.

"Well next time don't ask me a question that you don't want the answer to," Terrance said while laughing at Pistol Pete.

"Anyways, what did you do today?"

"Shit... me and your crazy sister and the kids went out to eat and to the water park for family day."

"You might as well go ahead and go back home my nigga."

"I want to Tee, but right now I am loving my freedom.   Anyways, get up pimp and meet me at the honeycomb hideout at 45."

THE CAMP5 CREW

As Terrance pulled up to the honeycomb hideout on the north side, Pistol Pete's Benz was already parked in the driveway. Terrance couldn't help himself admiring the way it was sitting so pretty on the 22-inch Forgiato rims, black on black.

"Damn bro that 550 looking sick out there right now," Pistol Pete said.

"Shit Tee... leave the keys to the Wraith and you can take it." The room got quiet. Then Terrance said, "see the way my bank account is set up.. I ahh..."

Everybody busted out laughing before Terrance could finish. They knew he was about to come up with some BS. The whole crew was there—James, Adrian, Jason and Jamal. This was the spot where they would come to kick it and talk about the past, present, and future.

The Sunday night game was on, Miami Dolphins against the Tampa Bay Buccaneers so everyone was drinking and talking shit. Tatiana and her home girls were over hanging out and drinking. Everybody in her damn crew was bad. Camp5 had a strict policy at the fun house—bad bitches only. No Dirty Foots allowed. That shit was for them niggas that was still on the block, chasing nickels and dimes. Camp5 Crew had graduated to the big leagues, like Meek Mills song says, "it's levels to this shit," and the Camp5 Crew was on the top level.

"Tee I almost forgot bro. Me and Tonya slid through Snatching earlier today to see what was popping, while the kids were in church with Grandma Joanne. When we rode through the four-way, this nigga Quick Money was all in my whip like he was riding in the passenger seat. I know you and Lucky Lefty got a red light on the beef, but buddy was looking like he was ready to do it. Had me paranoid and clutching," said Pistol Pete.

"The funny thing about that situation is Kay was telling me she bumped into them fools at the grocery store earlier," said Terrance. "She said Lucky was asking her questions about me and her and if we were still together."

"Well, that's very disrespectful," said Pistol Pete. "Do they need to be reminded of how we get down?"

"Not right now. We have too many power moves coming up in these next couple of months. We can't afford to put anything at risk," responded Terrance.

"I feel you, Tee. I just don't want these other crews thinking we are weak and vulnerable out here in these streets, you hear me?" said Pistol Pete.

"Perception is a big part of deception. As long as they are thinking we are losing our grip on the streets that leaves us with the edge on them. Chess my brother; we always play chess not checkers," Jamal replied.

After eating and watching the football game, the crew all went and sat in the oval room for the ritual Sunday meetings to discuss business for that week and next week. Jason ran the barbershops. James had the auto-body game on lock. Adrian and Jamal ran a fleet of 18 wheelers and Terrance and Pete were in the diamond business. They all had a hand in real estate. The crew had done very well for itself considering where they all had come from. The matter at hand tonight was Akeem flying in from Dubai. He was the new Middle East connect on the diamonds industry, very nice rocks for wholesale.

"Okay me and Adrian will meet up with Hector about the next shipment of product," Jamal added.

"Good," said Jason. My clientele is getting low out in Windermere, Florida. You know how Asian motherfuckers are about their product. They want it on time, every time." None of them moved product in the neighborhoods, after Johnny Blaze got knocked off with them 100 kilos. They all figured you shouldn't shit where you sleep. In other words, they didn't deal with the urban community ever since they had bad blood with the Down 4 Myne Crew a few years back. Shit got really messy...

So, the schedule was set for the coming week. Everyone was on point and ready to roll, business as usual... Terrance, Jason, and Jamal headed home to their family.

Chapter 6

Terrance arrived at the office refreshed and ready to work. The store was not open yet, but his employees were there setting the jewelry displays up for the day. Ms. Pat and Mr. Charles had been there ever since Terrance opened the first store in the flea market. He kept them on the team as managers when he purchased some real estate uptown and built a storefront.

Business was great so he hired more employees to work at the store, one Spanish chick named Rosalina and a white girl named Dianne.

Everyone was very attractive and business savvy, with great attitudes at "A-One Jewels." It was a great work environment, great pay, and full benefits.

As soon as Terrance sat down at his desk, Lisa walked in. "Are you ready for today Boss Man?"

Terrance immediately got an attitude. "Lisa, don't call me that shit."

Lisa busted out laughing, because she knew he didn't like being called Boss Man. That is what they had to call the prison guards when he was locked upstate for a year and a day.

"I was having a great morning until you came in here wanting to play. Nobody likes Mondays but you!"

"I love everyday Terrance, stop being a sour patch kid."

"Whatever Lisa. Let's get some work done," said Terrance. "So, what's on the agenda for today?"

"Well, you know you have that important meeting with Akeem at ten-thirty am. I have already set the conference room up. I just wanted to get you up to speed on everything else that we have planned for you today."

Akeem walked in dressed in a Thobe carrying a black leather duffle bag with his two brothers and four bodyguards. Everyone was introducing themselves except the bodyguards; they just stood there doing their surveillance of the store. Terrance could tell that they were making Pete nervous from the way that he was looking at them and them looking back at him. So, Terrance quickly defused the situation by saying, "Let's go and look at these beautiful jewels that you have brought to my country Akeem."

Sitting down at the conference table, Akeem opened up the bag and displayed the beautiful flawless diamonds on the tabletop. Today was all business, but Terrance couldn't help himself from noticing the diamond set. "How much for that set Akeem? That shit would look good on my baby Kay."

"This whole set goes for two million on the market, but for you I will do 300k," Akeem responded. "It's 100 karats Terrance, you can't beat it."

The set was amazing, the earrings were five karats a piece, the bracelet was 20 karats, the necklace was 50 karats, and the watch was 20 karats. Kay would die for this set and their 10-year anniversary was coming up so of course he made the purchase.

"Now where's the piece you promised me that I would love?" Akeem asked Terrance.

By the time Akeem and his brothers left the meeting, he was walking out with a healthy cashier check and seven million in cash. All together Terrance spent 19.5 million in one morning.

"Hell of a Monday, huh?" Lisa asked.

"Yes, it was. I haven't spent that much money at one time in a long time. It was a great investment; business is doing great. Now that we have new high-profile clients spending with us on a regular basis."

"Let's go to brunch. All this spending money has gotten me hungry as hell."

*   *   *

Jamal and Adrian were pulling up to the port of Tampa to meet up with Hector about the new shipment of coke that was supposed to be arriving. Things always ran smooth with Hector and the Mendez Cartel, but you can never be too careful with these crazy motherfuckers.

"What's going on amigos?" said Hector. "Where is Terrance?"

"He had some other obligations to take care of," said Adrian. "But he really wanted to be here and he sends his blessing, and payment."

"Speaking of payments, one of our east coast distributors got caught up in a little trouble and we don't trust his second in command. The guy is a total fuck up. So, we need your crew to move two hundred thousand pounds of high-grade marijuana for us. We will give it to you at $600 a pound."

"That's not what we do, Hector," said Jamal. "Plus, we need a chance to take it up with the rest of the crew..."

"Listen, amigo, I understand, but this is a one-time deal we are taking four hundred off each one. You guys stand to make mucho dinero off of this deal. I can have my guy make the delivery in the morning."

"Well shit... if you can give it to us for $500 a pound you have a deal," said Jamal. Hector agreed to the deal.

On the way back home, Jamal kept thinking about the deal he and Adrian made without the rest of the crew's consent, but he knew it was a great deal that anyone would have had problems passing on.

"What's wrong?" Adrian asked.

"Everything going to be alright. Trust these things seems to work themselves out. The rest of the guys know we wouldn't make a stupid move without them. The one thing this crew has is trust and a bunch of level headed men, none of us is making crazy moves out here in these streets. 100,000 kilos and 200,000 pounds of hydro. This is making out to be a beautiful week, and it's just Monday."

Chapter 7

Lucky pulled up to his trap to meet up with his crew, they had a lot that needed to be talked about. This month was really slow; the product wasn't as good as it usually is, and the Feds was on his trail. It was way too much for one person to think about. Quick Money was already there with the rest of the crew shooting dice when Lucky walked in.

"What's up Luck? Shit been crazy out here, Fox said." Fox felt like someone had been tailing him all week since his close call with the Narc boys.

"Everybody meet me in the basement. I have something I want to talk about," said Lucky.

Oh, shit the basement wasn't never good news. The crew knew something was up. Slim was nervous walking down the stairs, unsure if his cover had been blown or not. You could hear a church mouse. It was so quiet as everyone sat around waiting for Lucky Lefty to speak.

"Ok listen my nigga, this last month has been a real shitty one. The only thing good out of it is we have managed to maintain and our business is still intact. Quick, how many kilos do you and Fox have left?"

"Shit... Lucky, I am down to half a kilo, and I still got three out there on credit said," Quick Money.

"Alright what about you Fox?"

"To be honest Lucky, I still got five after last Saturday. I was afraid to move anything."

"It's better not to take a chance and go with your gut feelings than to be locked up. So, this is what we are going to do. Fox, give the rest of your work to Cory and Travis. You little niggas know what to do right?"

"Hell, yeah Lefty, we were trained for this moment. We were waiting to jump off the porch and play in the big leagues."

"Yeah Lucky.... we got the west side on lock," said Travis.

"Alight little niggas hold your horses. Fox I still want you to oversee this situation from afar though. We can't have any slip ups."

"No problem Lucky."

"Slim I need you to go and check the Jamaicans at the dread club. Find out what's taking them so long with that payment; it should be a brown bag". Quick Money's face bald, but he caught it before anyone else could notice it after Lucky Lefty's last request. "Alright guys so everybody knows what they need to do. I will hit yawl up when the next shipment touches down. Down 4 Myne, we all we got." The meeting was over.

"Quick, I need you to ride with me and check on something." Lucky Lefty and Quick Money jumped in his truck and rode off. Lucky Lefty poured a cup of cognac and lit up his cigar. He knew Quick was itching to know what was going on with the Jamaicans and Slim, Quick knew the meaning of the brown paper bag.

"So, Lucky what's going on with the dreads?" asked Quick?

"I stopped by Jackie's house the other day," responded Lucky.

"Jackie? Damn Luck you are a lucky cat to be fucking with that sexy ass woman."

Lucky smiled. He knew Quick Money was telling the truth about Jackie's fine ass! "Yeah Quick, I asked her to check out that situation with Fox and the Narc team. Come to find out this nigga Slim is a confidential informant."

"What this nigga Slim a snitch! Lucky let me kill that rat bitch!" said Quick.

"Ease up Quick. This has to be done the right way. We can't take that kind of heat right now, so it has to come from somewhere else, you feel me?"

"I just wish I could exterminate that rat bitch myself."

"Me too Quick, me too," said Lucky. "Speaking of Spanish girls, remember that girl I told you was working for that nigga Terrane jewelry store? She hit me today and said a lot of money and jewels were being moved around that establishment today and I mean a lot."

"What kind of numbers are we talking about quick?"

"Millions."

"Are you ready to lay them niggas down or what?"

"Not yet Quick. Everything must be on point and in order when we make that kind of move. Tee and his crew are not regular street thugs; they will be watching from every angle."

"Ok cool. I will just keep my chick in place with her eyes open to see what else she can find out that might be helpful."

"That sounds like a plan, my friend," Lucky replied with a smirk on his face.

Chapter 8

Terrance and Pistol Pete were finishing up brunch when his phone rings. "What's up baby, how is work going today?"

"It is going okay. I still have one more house to show and then I have this doctor's appointment at three pm. How did your meeting go this morning?" asked Kay.

"It went great. I purchased a lot of beautiful pieces that should turn a large profit."

"Well, that's good. I am proud of you baby. You have come a long way, and I can see the maturity in you now."

"Well thank you Miss Jones, I will continue to try my hardest to keep making you a proud wife."

"You are handsome, but first you have to marry me!" said Kay.

Jamal called Pistol Pete and asked him to meet at the warehouse. Something about a load coming in that needed to be second checked. Pistol Pete knew that was a code for we need to talk, something is not right.

"Tee you go ahead and take care of the rest of the store business and I am going to go and catch up with Jamal over at the warehouse to make sure everything went well with the shipment."

"Ok just hit me up if something's wrong then I will swing by."

"I can handle it. Just make sure you get that showcase setup. We spent a lot of money today," said Pete.

Pistol Pete pulled up to the warehouse off of Highway 98. Jamal and Adrian's semi-trucks were back in along with another one that Pistol Pete didn't recognize. A Spanish-driver was sitting in the truck.

"What's good Mal?" and Adrian. "Who is this guy in the truck?"

"One of Hector's east coast distributors ran into some trouble and he didn't trust his second in charge so he then offered us an opportunity to take his shipment at a price we couldn't beat. I was kind of hesitant at first, for the simple fact of when we make moves it's as a whole committee, no one man calls the shots, but Adrian helped me to see this was a great deal and opportunity for us!"

"So, what's in the package? More blows, pills or meth?"

"Hell no, it's high-grade marijuana, two hundred thousand pounds at $500 apiece. We stand to make one hundred million in profits, having to spend no upfront money."

"That sounds really good, but who do we get to move all this shit? We don't have any foot soldiers on the streets anymore. We gave that up after Blaze got knocked so we could look more legit. I was thinking we can use the Jamaicans network and let them flood the streets with the product."

"That's a big risk, Adrian. What if something goes wrong?"

"Me and Jamal already agreed to cover any losses out of our own pockets."

"Ok we will run this by the rest of the guys tonight at the honeycomb hideout for Monday night football," said Pistol Pete.

*   *   *

Terrance was sitting in his office going through his iMac looking for venues when Rosalina knocked on the office door. She was around the age of 22 still in college with the body of a goddess. Terrance knew she was trouble. A weak man would have slept with her, but Tee was all business; he knew the risk of sleeping with an employee, especially one that was this fine. Nevertheless, that didn't stop him from looking. She had the most amazing blue eyes. Rosalina looked like God had made her from a story book that came alive straight off of the pages.

"Boss Man, I was wondering if I could get off early Friday? I have tickets for the BiM Mathis and HB Murda concert."

Terrance responded, "Yes if you get me a ticket."

"Well, I didn't know you wanted to go. Let me call my connection and see what I can do," said Rosalina.

"No, you don't have to do that. I am just kidding. You can have the whole weekend off with pay and I will get you and your friends some VIP backstage tickets," said Terrance.

"For real Boss Man, you would do that for me?" asked Rosalina with excitement in her voice. She hugged Terrance and ran out of his office to call her friends.

"What was all that fuss about?" Lisa asked Terrance when she walked in his office.

"Nothing much. I just gave her the weekend off to go to the BiM Mathis and HB Murda concert," leaving out the part with pay, because Terrance knew Lisa would not agree with that choice.

Lisa frowned. Terrance noticed the look on her face and called her out on it. "Come on Lisa just because you are old fashioned doesn't mean you have the right to judge her."

"I am not judging anyone. Anyways... did you find a venue that you like or want to use?" asked Lisa. "Unlike Rosalina, I actually have to work."

"That was low Lisa!" said Terrance. No that was true, replied Lisa. Lisa just stood there staring at Terrance, Terrance broke the silence.

"I am looking at this place in downtown Miami. It's very elegant, and secure. Our clients can fly privately or commercially. And after shopping with us there's plenty of options when it comes to the nightlife in Miami, South Beach," said Terrance.

"I think that's a great idea. I will check the prices and availability of the other venues just in case the one you want is not available," replied Lisa. Instantly forgetting about the Rosalina situation for the moment.

"Ok Lisa, thank you. I don't know what I would do without you." Lisa rolled her eyes at Terrance and walked out of his office.

Chapter 9

Slim pulled into the dread club, and jumped out of his car. The reggae music was loud, and the smell of ganja was even louder. The old head Jamaicans were gambling playing Dominoes and the young ones were standing around hustling and drinking Guinness. Slim asked the dread named Tiger if the Jamaican Key-tee was around and Tiger pointed at the privacy fence behind the building.

Slim opened the gate and went inside the privacy fence. As soon as the gate closed behind him, two shots rang out BANG, BANG! Three more shots BANK, BANG, BANG! As Slims lifeless body laid on a plastic bag that was about ten feet long and ten feet wide, Key-Tee stood over him talking in his Jamaican slang, "Pussy Claud's informant, the boy then dead!"

He called Lefty Lucky, "Yo my youth good doing business with you I receive your brown paper bag."

Lucky smiled and hung up the phone. He was at the mall shopping with Tracey. "Damn bae why are you smiling and shit? That better not be a female calling you!"

"Chill out Tracy, that was a bad business deal that got corrected. Let's go and celebrate whatever you want to do!"

"Whatever I want to do?"

"Yes, that's what I said!"

"Ok let's start with me sucking on you on the way to Hot and Juicy Crawfish."

"Talking like that we won't make it to Hot and Juicy."

"Oh, we are going to Hot and Juicy and I am going to suck that all the way there," said Tracy. Quick Money and one of his random chicks at the moment met Lucky Lefty and Tracy at the restaurant. Tracy rolled her eyes at the girl when Quick Money introduced her. She could care less about one of Quick Money's random chicks.

"When was the last time you talked to Aisha?" Tracy asked Quick Money, trying to be funny. Aisha was her best friend, so Tracy knew they were not talking at the moment.

"Come on Tracy with the BS you're tripping," said Quick Money.

"I was just asking nigga, damn my bad!" said Tracy. Lucky told Tracey to chill out and stop being messy. The girl Quick Money was with didn't care about Tracy's pettiness. She was only there for some free seafood and a little shopping. She knew the beat between her and Quick Money.

"Anyways Quick Money that brown paper bag got delivered today."

"What! For real? Man are we celebrating tonight? Everything is on me! Let's hit up club Lux."

"I can't brother. I promised Tracy we were doing whatever she wanted to do."

"That's right Quick, he is all mine tonight," said Tracy.

"Well sister, you two enjoy the rest of your day. Me and Shante are going to hit the mall, blow a bag, and explore the city tonight. Hit me up if you two lames decide that you want to have some fun."

"Ok my brother from another mother, be safe out there on the streets," Lucky added.

"Always do, Down 4 Myne Team, we all we got." Quick Money left the restaurant.

Tracy finished up with her king crabs and grilled shrimp, baked potato, and washed it down with her third Long Island Iced Tea. "Damn bae I am full and tipsy."

"So, what do you have planned for us to do next?"

"I was thinking we should Netflix and Chill."

"Sounds like a plan to me. Let's get home ASAP before you change your mind," said Lucky Lefty.

*   *   *

"Fuck! Something is not right," said Detective Smith. "This is not like Slim. He usually reports every 12 hours."

"Maybe he decided to run," said Detective Jones. "You can never trust a rat."

"No, the deal we are giving him is too sweet for anyone to run. Let's go to plan B. Activate his GPS chip. We need to track him before it's too late. I got a bad feeling about this."

The technician told Detective Jones that Slims GPS is showing that he is in the sugar cane fields off of Highway 27 near the Everglades. Detective Smith called in a favor with Sgt. Jackson from South Bay Florida.

"Well, it's not good. We have a deceased black male here with three bullet holes in his body and two in his head."

"Ok we will be there to identify the body," said Detective Smith. "Fuck!" Detective Jones flipped over the table, coffee and paperwork flew everywhere.

Chapter 10

Terrance pulled up to his house around five-thirty in the afternoon. Pistol Pete's car was parked in the guest house driveway, so he decided to text him to meet him in the backyard to talk while he fed the dogs.

"So, what's the deal Pete? Everything good with the shipment?"

"Yeah, Hector just dropped some extra work on us. One of his east coast distributors ran into some trouble with the law and he didn't trust his second in charge with that much work, so he asked us to take it."

Terrance laughed and said, "That Chico Hector is paranoid as hell, so how much was it?"

Pistol Pete told Tee it was two hundred thousand pounds of hydro marijuana.

"Shit bro that's a lot of fucking weed. What's the ticket?"

"Five hundred apiece."

"Okay we will address that tonight with the rest of the crew."

Kay came out of the back-sliding door. "What's up baby boy?"

Talking to her younger brother Pete. "When are you going to go back home to Tonya?" asked Kay. "These damn kids need you there for real!"

"Ease up baby," said Terrance. "How did your doctor's appointment go?"

"It went well. The doctor said everything looks normal," said Kay.

"Wait a minute Kay are you sick or something?" asked Pistol Pete.

"No fool, you are about to be an uncle."

"Oh, shit congratulations sister. Damn Tee, you weren't going to tell me?"

"I didn't want to jinx anything before she went to the doctor today."

"Damn bruh I am excited for you two!" said Pete.

"We are having steaks, potatoes, and salad tonight. Are you eating with us Pete?"

"Hell, yeah sis we are celebrating our new edition to the family."

"So how was your day at work Kay? Did you sell any houses?" asked Terrance.

"Yes, I sold that four bedroom, three and a half bath on the next block off of Lincoln Street to a Jewish lawyer and his family. I made a 65-thousand-dollar commission off it."

"Damn Kay I am proud of you baby!"

"Yes, I will try. So how did things go in the meeting this morning with your new diamond supplier?" Kay asks Terrance and Pete.

"We invested a lot of bread, now we are just setting up the venue to have the showcase for all of our high-end customers that spend hundreds of thousands of dollars on jewelry," said Terrance.

"Where are you thinking about getting the venue at?" asked Kay.

"I was thinking about doing one in each major city: Los Angeles, Atlanta, Miami, and New York. That way we can give our clients a different type of feel."

"I think that's a great idea honey."

"Me too, Dawg. You need to run that through Lisa and get her on its ASAP."

Later on in the evening, they all sat around the dinner table.

"Kay this steak tastes great! You cook like Mama and Grandma. Keep feeding me like this and I might not ever want to leave," said Pistol Pete.

"Whatever nigga you taking your ass back home soon. You only have nine more months," said Kay.

"Ease up bae. Bruh you can stay here as long as you need to," said Terrance!

"Thanks Tee!" Pistol Pete replied. "I am about to go and take a shower. I will meet you at the spot for Monday night football."

"Okay Pete. I need to get a shower too. I will meet you there around eight-thirty."

Terrance was getting out of the shower drying off when Kay asked him if he would be out late.

"I will be back around one if that's not too late for you?" said Terrance.

"No, that's cool. Tonya is coming over with the kids. We are going to watch Basketball Wives and Love and Hip-Hop tonight!"

"I don't know why you two love all that drama television," Terrance responded to the reality TV BS that Kay loves watching.

Kay shot back fast by saying, "I don't know why you guys love to see men tackling one another on grass."

"Because it's a violent sport baby," replied Terrance.

"Whatever, give me a kiss and be safe," said Kay.

"See you later, love." Terrance walked out of the room...

Chapter 11

Detective Jones and Detective Smith pulled up to the cane field in South Bay Florida to identify the deceased male. It was Slim for sure. Jones just shook his head. "Smith, looks like a professional hit," said Sgt. Jackson.

"Yeah, you two got a shit fest here son." After all night of pleading with the head state prosecutor, Detective Smith got her to pull a bullshit warrant on Fox. They knew it would not stick, but they needed to know how much he knew about Slims homicide. Fox was pulling up to his house when a swat team jumped out on him.

"Freeze, get your hands up and get on the ground, you piece of shit! You are under arrest." Fox immediately got on the ground he knew Highlands County Sheriff's Office would not hesitate to shoot him.

"What did I do man? Yawl don't have anything on me."

"Just shut the fuck up, and put your hands behind your back," said Detective Jones.

They took Fox into custody at the county jail after booking him in for conspiracy to sell cocaine. They took him straight from booking to the investigation room and started asking him questions about Slim and their relationship with each other.

"Slim? I know him from seeing him around, but that's about it," Fox responded. Fox wheels in his head were turning fast as hell, and his heart was about to jump out of his chest; it was beating ten times faster than normal. He knew Slim was a snitch. He tried to tell Lucky Lefty this shit but he wouldn't listen to him. Now he was on his way up the creek without a paddle for a fucking rat!

Sitting in the small investigation room by himself, all kinds of thoughts were running through Fox's head. After forty-five minutes of sitting alone in that small room, Detective Jones and Smith walked in, one of them holding a green folder filled with papers. Detective Jones dropped the folder in front of Fox and told him to open it. Fox hesitated at first, then he opened it. On the front page was a picture of a deceased. Slim laying in what looked like a sugar cane field. His body was filled up with bullet holes. Fox immediately started smiling on the inside he knew this case of conspiracy on him was as dead as Slim was!

"Ok what the hell! What's the meaning of this? Why in the hell you two pricks showing this to me?" asked Fox. "I have nothing to do with this, nor do I know anything about it. I would like to speak to my lawyer please. Can you two please take me back to my cell? I should be bonding out of your establishment real soon," said Fox. Fox had a new burst of confidence after seeing them files. Detective Smith knew for sure Fox had nothing to do with Slim's murder. His body language was too relaxed. He seemed to be relieved that Slim was dead, like a burden had been lifted off of his shoulders. They escorted Fox back to his cell. Kim bonded him out the same night on the conspiracy charge.

When Fox got in the car with Kim, he started laughing. She was wondering what the hell was wrong with him. He seems to be really happy for a man that was just bailed out of jail, for conspiracy to sell coke.

"What's going on baby? Why are you so happy?" asked Kim.

The Feds brought me in on a bogus charge. Hoping that I knew something about Slims murder."

"Hold on so you are telling me that Slim is dead?" asked Kim.

"Hell yes, somebody smoked that fool and left his body laid in the cane fields down in the muck. Without that rat, they don't have a case on me baby. I need to call Lucky Lefty and the rest of the crew. They need to know what's going on."

"Damn baby you dodged a bullet. I keep telling you to be safe out there in these streets. People will do anything to save themselves," said Kim.

Lucky was sound asleep when his phone rang at three-thirty in the morning. If it wasn't for Tracy, he would have ignored it. "Fuck this better be urgent. Hello!"

It was Fox's voice. "Wake up Luck, and open the door. I am outside."

Lucky could hear the urgency in Fox's tone. "Okay I am coming right now," replied Lucky.

"What's wrong?" Tracy asks Lucky.

"I don't know. Your crazy ass cousin, Fox, is outside. He sounds shaken up about something." Lucky Lefty got up and slipped on some shorts and went to open the door. Tracy put on a nightgown and went into the kitchen to fix some hot tea.

"Do you want some hot tea?"

"No thanks. We are going out back to the game room," said Lucky.

Lucky poured two glasses of cognac one for him and one for Fox and then lit up a cigar. "So, what's so urgent you couldn't wait until the sun came up to stop by or call me?"

"Man Lucky, I just got out of central booking."

"What the hell were you doing in central booking Fox?" ask Lucky.

"I went into my house about eight o'clock yesterday. Out of nowhere the S.O.U., and Swat Team jumped out and took me to jail for conspiracy to sell cocaine." Lucky Lefty eyebrows lifted up to show concern about the charges that they were trying to pin on Fox.

"They took me straight from booking to this investigation room and started to question me about Slim. I knew for sure I was done once they started asking me questions about that rat. Then the most beautiful thing happened. They showed me some pictures of Slim stretched out in the cane field. He must have really pissed somebody off!" said Fox.

"So, you are telling me that Slim is dead and they found his body?" asked Lucky.

"Yes, cousin, that is exactly what I am saying!"

"Did they say if they had any other leads?" asked Lucky.

"No, they were pressing me for information, but I immediately asked for my lawyer," said Fox.

"You did good, Fox. You did really well," said Lucky.

Lucky Lefty had no intention of telling Fox that he was the one that ordered the hit on Slim. The less he knew the better things were for the both of them.

Chapter 12

Captain Rogers walked in the break room, where the two detectives were sitting drinking coffee. "I heard you boys had a rough night last night. I heard that you lost a star witness in the Down 4 Myne Crew case Captain Rogers" asked the two detectives with a stern voice. "Yes, Captain we are in the middle of a shit storm right now" they responded. "It is okay boys. We all have lost key witnesses in cases. Go home and get some rest. Take you two days off and clear up your heads. I want you two guys to come back refreshed and ready to lock these thugs up. No more excuses" said Captain Rogers. "Yes, sir Captain", Detective Jones got up and left out the room. Detective Smith got up and followed behind him.

*   *   *

The week was going by slowly for Rosalina. The weekend could not get here fast enough. She was laying in her bed watching television when Quick called her. "What's up baby girl what are you up to?" "Nothing much just watching television, bored, what about you?" asked Rosalina? "Shitted. I am at the crib thinking about you. Do you want me to send an Uber to come and get you?" asked Quick Money. Today was Tuesday no street crews made moves on Tuesday it was more of a chill and reflective day for the true hustlers. "Yes, that's cool. Do you want me to bring clothes, and stay with you tonight? Because I have to work in the morning," said Rosalina. Quick didn't care if she stayed the rest of the week, He was missing her little tight vagina, so he was game to have her stay all night. "Is that even a question, pretty girl? Hell yes! I want you to stay tonight," said Quick Money. Thirty minutes later Quick's doorbell rang. It was Rosalina. Who was looking sexy as ever with her all black lace dress on. Quick wasted no time taking Rosalina against the wall and pushing his manhood inside her. He had forgotten how good she was. He had forgotten how wet she got. After seven or eight minutes, Quick was exploding all over Rosalina. "Damn baby that Puerto Rican candy is so damn good! So how are things working out with your new job?" Quick asked.

"Everybody there is very polite to me except for Lisa. She is a stuck-up bitch. I think she is jealous of me," Rosalina told Quick Money, referring to Lisa.

"Well baby you have to be careful with her. She watches Tee's back like a hawk. Anything suspicious, she will notice it," said Quick Money. "So again, make sure you are extra careful around her."

"Don't worry about her, I got this," Rosalina told Quick Money with a smile on her face that made Quick Money horny for the second round.

*   *   *

Sitting in his office, Terrance couldn't help thinking about his unborn child, marrying Kay and getting the hell out of the game for good. The other night he told the crew that he was close to retiring and going all the way legit, and they should be thinking the same way. Terrance knew the crew was blessed to last this long without any major setbacks besides Blaze getting knocked, everyone else was alive, free and well. After the showcases and this batch of products gets sold. This was it for Tee. The plan was to cash everyone out and go his separate way. Terrance knew Pistol Pete wasn't going to be happy. But that didn't matter because Terrance had a kid to look after now. Jamal knew something was up when Terrance told them to keep all the profit from the weed and split it up between the crew! It was just time to go straight and everyone knew it. You can say it was like the elephant in the room at every meeting. But it was time.

The telephone rings. Terrance answers. Lisa says, "I have D-Money's manager on line one."

"Okay patch him through," Terrance instructed Lisa. "What's good Cuzin Joe? It's been a minute since I heard from you. We got some catching up to do. Can you meet me for a quick lunch? I will send a car to get you," said Terrance.

Capitol Grill had some great food on the menu but Terrance only had a salad and crab cakes. It was too early to eat heavy. Cuzin Joe orders a full course meal. He knew he wouldn't get another chance to eat again. The music Industry always kept him so busy to ever have any real time to himself. Terrance pulled out the custom piece and placed it on the table. It was a rose gold and hand draped in flawless VVS diamonds. Just the pendant alone was worth 350k. Joe was the homie, so he only charges him 275k, plus the VIP backstage passes for Rosalina and her home girls.

After catching up at lunch with Cuzin Joe, Terrance headed back to the office to finish up the rest of the work day. Lisa was busy closing the deal on all of the venues and so far, everything was going as planned; the schedule was set and ready to go. Terrance called Rosalina into his office to give her the backstage passes for the concert. She was very excited. On her way out the door she turned around and said, "Boss Man if you need anything from me... I mean anything, just ask."

Terrance knew what she was getting at and maybe a few years back he would have taken her up on that offer; but, not now he was too dedicated to his woman and running his business to play those types of games with any other woman. Pistol Pete walked into Terrance's office.

"Brother look! I know you are ready to go straight but I still need you. I can't do this without you! We are a team that is how we came in as a team."

Terrance looked Pistol Pete in his eyes and said, "Well brother that's the way we should go out. As a team. And I say it's time to get out. We have enough money to do whatever we want. It's time to go legit there is no other way around it," said Terrance.

Pistol Pete knew he was not changing Terrance's mind on this one, so he gave Tee a handshake and a hug before he walked out of Terrance's office. "I love you man. You are a brother that I never had and always wanted."

"I love you, Pete. That's why it's time to switch up our game before our time runs out."

*   *   *

Black Boy was sitting in the barber chair at Magazine Ready Barbershop getting a fade when Frank walked in. Frank was the neighborhood news reporter. This guy knew everyone's business and was always 99% accurate on his information. "Vee, did you hear about Slim from Belle Glade?" Vee was the owner of Magazine Ready Barbershop.

"No, what happened to him?"

"Word, is they found that boy with two in the head and three in the chest. They say Lucky Lefty and the dreads had something to do with it" Frank continued to tell Vee. Black Boy was quietly listening to Frank spill the beans, but he never gave any input because if any of this was true that Frank was reporting to Vee, a war in the streets was on its way for sure.

After Black Boy got out of the chair he paid Vee for his haircut, and dapped everybody up on the way out. Frank said, "Let me holla at you for a minute Black." Frank and Black walked outside, Frank told Black Boy, "Look I know you fuck with the dreads heavy, but that nigga Slim was connected. If any of this is true, shit is about to get really ugly really fast."

Black told Frank, "Do you remember last New Year's at that famous rapper strip party when the niggas ran in there and laid everything and everybody down. Killed four niggas and three bitches? That was Slim's cousin and his crew. They called them niggas The Muck Boys. Word on the streets, they called them niggas the body snatchers. I used to see Slim from time to time," said Black Boy. "And every time he would tell me I am about tired of sparing these fuck niggas, but you good Black. I always thought you were a solid dude. Those were his exact words. So, if what you are saying is true, I am about to lay low cause the streets are about to get really bloody," said Black Boy.

"Word." Frank gave Black Boy a handshake and went back into the barber shop.

Chapter 13

Word got back to Freddy that someone had killed his favorite cousin Slim. Freddy knew Slim was a snitch but that didn't change the fact that Slim had saved his life more than once. Juan was Freddy's right-hand man and he knew how much Slim had meant to Freddy. "Don't worry my nigga. We are going to give everyone involved a slow painful death," said Juan.

"Just relax. I got Ralph and Willie gathering intel for us right now in Highlands County. If they find anything fishy. We are going to turn that shit upside down." Freddy was smoking a blunt and sitting on his porch. The only thing he could think about was his cousin and all the good times they had together. Slim was always a gangster but his loyalty to the wrong people always got him into sticky situations. Slim and Freddy's mom were twin sisters and they were both in the house taking it hard. Freddy couldn't take all the sadness so he jumped on the ATV and hit the cane fields. As he pulled up to the spot where they found Slims' body, tears started running down his face as he looked up to the sky. At that moment, he made a promise to Slim that everyone involved would pay for his death with their own life.

Ralph and Willie were on the block in Avon Park talking to Jamaican Wayne about some work. They knew if they just went in asking questions about Slim it would raise too many eyebrows and their orders were to stay as low key as possible. Ralph and Willie were Freddy's best soldiers.

They followed Juan's orders to the T. Everything needed to be by the book. This was personal. Plus, they knew if they messed this up, it was a possibility they could end up in a hole right next to the cowards that did this to Slim. Wayne was telling Ralph that he knew someone that just got a lot of good trees in and was looking to expand. The link up might be good for everybody. He just needed a few hours and he would get back to them.

Adrian pulled up on Jamaican Key-Tee at the dread club. Usually, he would not take a risk like this but he knew Key-Tee had the manpower to move his product faster than anyone else on the streets. Jamaican Key-Tee was a shooter with mad respect on the streets. Adrian knew no one would be foolish enough to try and rob Key-Tee for a product. The problem was the heat that Key-Tee brought on from the police and rival crews. Key-Tee had left more bodies in his path than the Crip Keeper himself. Adrian gave Key-Tee one thousand pounds of loud and five days to get rid of it. This was more than enough time for the most feared dread in Florida. Jamaican Wayne met up with Key-Tee to buy ten pounds of loud. Key-Tee told him two thousand four hundred apiece. Wayne made the purchase without blinking an eye. He knew that it was a very sweet deal for this good of a product. Ralph and Willie were following Wayne the whole time without being noticed. They knew he knew something plus they were looking to rob Wayne and whoever he was getting his work from.

After talking to Key-Tee, Jamaican Wayne pulled off. Willie pulled out three cars behind him being cautious as ever not to get notice. Wayne was driving carefully down

Highway 27. Never doing more than five miles over the speed limit. After about ten minutes, Wayne pulled into a community named Sun n' Lakes. The houses were nice and low key and back in a wooded area. This was perfect for what Ralph and Willie had planned next. Ralph called Jamaican Wayne to ask him what was up with the play. Wayne told him he needed an hour or so and everything was a go. By this time, Freddy and Juan were coming through Lake Placid. Freddy couldn't sit on the sidelines any longer. He needed answers about Slims' death.

As soon as Jamaican Wayne walked out of his house, he felt a hard object hit him across his head and then another. "Bombard clot!" screamed Wayne. He was pistol-whipped and dragged back into his house by two men dressed in all black. The lights were bright, his ears were ringing and his vision was blurry as Wayne came back to his senses. He recognized Ralph and Willie, standing over him.

"Yo! My boy is you robbing me for ten petty pounds of weed? Ah suh yah guh do mi?"

Out of nowhere two more figures appear. At that moment, Wayne knew this was not a robbery but something much different than that. "So, what have you come to kill me?"

Now that all depends on you and the information you give us Mr. Wayne," Freddy said in a soft but stern voice.

"And who are you supposed to be?" asked Wayne.

Before he could finish the sentence, Juan hit him in the mouth with the butt of his pistol. Blood flew everywhere. "Now we can do this the hard way or the harder way. Either way, I am leaving with the information I want tonight," said Freddy.

"My youth I didn't have any information. I am not an informer." Freddy and the crew laughed.

"Oh. You think we are the police huh? No. We are something much worse than that. I need some information about a murder."

"What murder? I haven't murdered anyone," replied Jamaican Wayne.

"Have you ever heard of Slim? He ran with a crew called Down 4 Myne. You know Lucky Lefty and them?" Jamaican Wayne knew exactly who Freddy was talking about. The snitch that Jamaican Key-Tee killed the other day at the dread club.

"No man. Me not know nothing about this." Juan struck Wayne again. Blood was pouring non-stop out of Wayne's head. They beat and tortured Wayne for an hour and a half before he finally gave up Key-Tee's name. Willie grabbed the ten pounds of weed and the money out of Wayne's safe. On the way out, Freddy looked at Juan and told him to finish it. Juan cut Wayne's throat from ear to ear and put one in his head to make sure the job was done.

Chapter 14

Lucky Lefty and Quick Money were sitting at the bar inside Applebee's restaurant having some lunch and a few drinks catching up on sports. The local news channel Fox 13 was reporting on the murder of Jamaican Wayne. Quick Money and Lucky were shocked about Mr. Wayne's murder. Who would want that nice guy gone they thought to themselves? Lucky decided to tell Quick about the run in that Fox had with the authorities last night. As usual, Quick Money overreacted until Lucky explained the whole situation to him. After that he calm down a little.

"So Lucky, what's our next play? We have to make something happen soon. Our supply is getting low and our connection just got knocked off." Lucky Lefty knew that Quick Money was right. He had been trying to figure out the same thing ever since the Palm Beach plug got arrested. There were not many options left on the table. It was looking like the only way to stay afloat was to set the plan in motion on Tee and his crew.

Lucky asked Quick if Rosalina had found out any more valuable information that they could use against their rival crew. None of them had any idea where Tee lived. That dude moved around like a ghost and was always switching cars. Terrance's way of thinking was total paranoia and total awareness. Even if his enemies did find out where he lived, it would not matter, his house was like a fortress—booby-traps everywhere.

"Rosalina is on her job, but shit is not moving fast enough. Maybe she needs to give that nigga some pussy or something to try and get his mouth to loosen up," Quick Money suggested.

"No, that won't work. Tee is not a sucker. He is way too intelligent for that move. She would only expose herself by taking that angle," said Lucky Lefty. "Maybe I have another way. Just keep her in the position that she is in, while I work on this other angle."

*   *   *

Lisa was way more than just Terrance's Executive Assistant. They came up together as kids. Raised up on the same street corner and played ball together until the streetlights came on and it was time to go home before dark caught you. (If you are from the hood you know exactly what I am talking about!) Lisa was always pretty growing up; she just had a tomboy edge to her. Hell, she was tougher than most of the boys! Lisa and Terrance were twelve when they shared their first kiss. It was awkward because neither one knew what they were doing. That was as far as it ever went between them, but they were always together. They share everything with one another. Everyone in high school thought that they had something going on, even Terrance's older sister Tonya. Kay used to get jealous of their relationship when she and Terrance first started dating but she got used to it really fast once she realized Lisa wasn't going anywhere. Before she and Lisa got cool, Lisa used to tell Terrance all the time, "Tell that bitch to quit rolling her eyes before she knocked them the fuck out".

Terrance always just laughed it off. He knew Kay couldn't stand in the paint with Lisa, but Kay never backed down which turned Terrance on in a weird sick way. Lisa was sitting in her office finishing up on her conference calls with the different venues, when Rosalina passed by her door leaving Terrance's office. Lisa frowned up. It was something about that fake Spanish bitch that just didn't sit well with her and she was going to get to the bottom of it. She waited ten minutes and buzzed the front of the store. "Mr. Charles, can you please send Rosalina to my office?"

"Yes, Lisa I will," said Mr. Charles.

On the way to Lisa's office, Rosalina was wondering what this evil woman could possibly want with her. She already knew Lisa didn't like her. That was obvious. Rosalina knew this summons couldn't be good.

Rosalina knocks on the door. "Come in," Lisa told Rosalina. "And have a seat."

Lisa knew Rosalina would be on high alert and have her guard up so she decided to take a different approach. "I hear you got the weekend off and some backstage tickets for the BiM Mathis and HB Murda concert."

Rosalina responded with a yes, at the same time thinking *damn, Terrance told this bitch everything*!

"Well, we have some very important showcases coming up next month and I wanted to know if you could use some extra cash working and hosting them? We could always use some extra eye candy to go along with our accessories we are selling. There will be a lot of important people there and a great chance for you to network and get your feet wet."

Rosalina couldn't believe how nice Lisa was being to her. Rosalina smiled with excitement and gladly accepted the invitation.

"Okay great," Lisa said. "So, I will have Ms. Pat put you on the travel list and have her set up a dinner date for us so I can go over more of the details about what the company will be expecting of you." Rosalina left the office smiling from ear to ear.

Lisa knew what she was doing. The best way to catch the fish you wanted is to find out what bait they can't resist. An old trick she learned from the neighborhood that she and Terrance grew up in.

Chapter 15

It was Thursday morning. The Highlands County Sheriff's office was busy and everyone was scrambling around. The hotlines were buzzing with all types of information coming in about Jamaican Wayne's murder. Detective Smith was sitting at his desk overlooking the Down 4 Myne Crew case trying to find out how his CI Slim got made. Detective Smith knew it had to be an internal leak in his task force. They were always careful when they met up with Slim. Someone had to be talking on the inside.

Detective Jones walked into Jackie's office. "How are you doing this morning, Officer Diaz?" Jackie was looking as beautiful as she always did. She knew Detective Jones had the hots for her. He is where she was getting all of her information from to keep Kenny and his crew of thugs
   out of central booking.

"I am doing great. How is this blessed day treating you my shining knight in armor? I hope you are keeping our streets safe?" Jackie knew how to play on a man's ego. She was undercover inside one of the most dangerous Mexican Cartels for three years. Someone like Detective Jones was easy pickings for her.

Captain Rogers called a mandatory meeting at nine hundred sharp in the main conference room. When Detective Jones walked in, he was surprised to see the DEA, U.S. Marshals, ATF and everyone from the task force all in one room. Things had gotten out of hand.

It was time for the authorities to lock these criminals up and take the streets back with all the necessary force. The community was in an uproar for peace in the neighborhood. One of the U.S. Marshals asked Detective Smith if he knew that there was a leak in his department, and what measures he was taking to seal that hole up as quickly as possible.

Detective Smith immediately went on the defense. "I don't need you fucking pricks coming into my department pointing fingers. If you did your fucking jobs at the borders, we wouldn't have these problems in the first place," said Detective Smith.

"Calm down, everybody calm down!

We are on the same team here. The enemy is out there," said Captain Rogers. "We won't get anywhere fighting amongst one another."

The DEA agent said, "I think we have another player in the game. A guy by the name of Terrance Young. We can never catch him with his hand in the cookie jar but we know he is a big fish out here."

Detective Jones spoke up. "This guy Terrance is so clean he doesn't even have a traffic ticket. Plus, he has a team full of powerful lawyers on his payroll. Terrance Young runs a diamond company downtown and is a lavish party planner to the stars. I don't know if you really want to be stirring up that ant bed." DEA knew all of that because they already had an undercover agent in place within Terrance's company gathering Intel. So far, the guy was clean as a whistle. No mistakes had been made. Either way, he was really good or not dirty at all. The meeting went on for two and a half hours. By the time it was over, it was lunch time. Everyone left the meeting on the same page, with one agenda, to take down the Down 4 Myne Crew and solve these murders.

At lunch Detective Jones and Detective Smith sat talking about the U.S. Marshal's and how cocky the pricks were. They knew that they had dropped the ball with Slim and that forced Captain Rogers hand to bring in help from outside agencies. But for Detective Smith and Jones this fight was personal. No way were they going to let the DEA or the U.S Marshals come in and take over their show.

U.S. Marshal Douglas and his partner headed to internal affairs to check out the leads on the investigation of the department. They knew there were some dirty cops in the Highlands County Sheriff's Office. On the way down the hall, Marshal Douglas heard a familiar voice call his name, "Tommy long time no see."

He knew that voice from anywhere. It was the beautiful Jackie Diaz. They had a fling back when she was still working for the FBI. Work kept them both too busy for it to lead to anything serious. Jackie was more wrapped up in her work back then. Tommy would have quit the U.S. Marshals for her.

"Wow Jackie you are still as stunning as I remember you! I swear you don't look a day older than you did when we were together."

"Oh, we were together?" asked Jackie.

"Woman, you know I was in love with you. You broke my heart for that Mexican cartel boss Don Omegas you were dating for three years."

"Now you know that was just part of the job Tommy," said Jackie.

"I know, but it still hurts! Well for what it's worth, we got that son of a bitch. I thought I lost you at one point. I sat beside your bed for three days praying you pulled through after he shot you. I only left your side when they said that they had found Don Omegas hideout. I had to go put a bullet in that fucker head personally."

"Aww that's so sweet. So, what are you guys doing in my neck of the woods?"

"Oh, damn...I am being so rude. Jackie Diaz, my partner Steve Anderson. Steve Anderson this is the beautiful Jackie Diaz." They shook hands. "We are here to take down Kenny Thomas and his Down 4 Myne crew. Have you ever heard of them guys?"

"As a matter of fact, I have. They have a reputation around these parts," said Jackie. So why are you guys in internal affairs snooping around? You should be in the Narcotics Division, right?" asked Jackie.

"Because someone is leaking out information in the Task Force department. We would like to find out who it is so we can nail the son of a bitches," said Marshal Douglas.

"Oh! I see. Well, it's good to see you again. Maybe we can catch up sometime over dinner," said Jackie.

Tommy smiled. "That would be nice. It was good seeing you. He gave Jackie a kiss and went up the elevator.

Jackie hurried back to her office and shut the door. She knew if they had called in Tommy Douglas that Kenny and his crew were in really big trouble. Tommy was the guy that always got his mark. She was trying to figure out a way to warn Kenny about the new threat that was looking at his front door without incriminating herself. Wondering how she even got caught up with this fool? The truth was ever since she went undercover, she still had an urge to be with a bad guy. She wasn't even mad at Don Omegas for shooting her. She felt like she had betrayed him by taking his empire down. After three years of being with someone every day, learning who they are, learning their deepest thoughts and learning that they are way more than the monster that you thought they were. You have a different outlook. Going undercover is a thin line between good and evil. if you are not careful, you can find yourself in too deep.

Chapter 16

The time was around nine o'clock a.m. Black Boy was at the neighborhood store named Leroy's. He'd seen this all-black Tahoe pass by like four times. Black Boy knew it wasn't the police unless they had added a new vehicle to their fleet of undercover cars. This was some jack boys looking to rob or something much worse. Maybe Slims' family from the Muck. The last domino hit the table when Black Boy's partner said, "Game over. Pay up. That's double."

Black collected his part of the winnings and said, "I am out fellas. I have a little business to take care of."

"Damn Black we're hot right now," said Curt.

"I will be back. Just hold it down. Give me like thirty minutes."

"Man, that nigga is not coming back," said one of the losers from the other team. Black Boy just kept walking. He was trying to make it to his car before the Tahoe got into the store parking lot. No one else noticed what was going down but him and an old head sitting around watching the dominos game.

Black Boy was just about to open his car door when a Chevy Tahoe slid up on him. Black started reaching for his pistol when a voice out of the truck said, "I don't think you want to do that playboy!"

When Black turned around a Spanish Guy with a mouth full of gold teeth had an AR-15 pointed at his face. The back window of the Tahoe rolled down. All

Black Boy could see is dark shades and dreadlocks through all the smoke coming out of the window. Finally, Fred said, "Black Boy get in the truck. I need to ask you a few questions about some pressing matters. This won't take long at all."

Black Boy started to weigh out his options. He knew if they wanted him dead all they had to do was shoot. If they wanted to rob him, they would have done that too by now. This had to be Slims' cousin, Infamous Freddy, the head of the dangerous Muck Boys Crew. Black Boy took his hand off of his pistol and jumped in the back seat of the truck. "Good choice," Juan told Black Boy as he was sitting down, Fred asked Black Boy to relax. This wasn't about him unless he didn't tell them the information they needed to know.

"Look I know you work for Jamaican Key-Tee and his crew. My cousin Slim told me a lot about you and it was all good. But right now, this situation is all bad. I hate to involve you but it is what it is," Fred told Black Boy. "Now what I am going to need from you is a complete layout of Key-Tee's operation. I want to know how he moves and why he moves every single detail."

Black Boy knew this was a double edge sword no matter which side he fell on. He was guaranteed to get cut. Jamaican Key-Tee was a bad man. He also knew Freddy and his crew had no morals. These niggas nick names were body snatchers for crying out loud! Black Boy palms were sweating; he knew he had to think fast. He told Freddy that he would cooperate. He just needed a couple of days to make sure he got all the details right.

Freddy agreed to give Black Boy the days besides he had a few things to look into before they made the move on Kay-Tee. Juan threw a Gucci duffle bag on Black Boy's lap. Freddy said, "That's five pounds of loud marijuana for your troubles. Save your bread up. You're going to need a new connection pretty soon." Black Boy jumped out the truck and right before he could shut the door, Freddy handed him a picture of his child's mother and son. "If you can't do this for me, at least do this for them, you dig?" Black Boy knew he was fucked!

*   *   *

Lisa pulled up to the restaurant in her 2023 Bentley Continental GT Range and valet parked it. Rosalina was already there in the waiting area outside. She took an Uber to get there. Lisa was twenty minutes late but that was part of her plan. Rosalina would be waiting and watching to see what she pulled up in. Lisa got out of the car, took the valet ticket and started walking towards the restaurant. Rosalina was not gay at all but when she saw Lisa walking... It's like time completely stopped. Lisa had on an all-black one-piece Versace dress that came about med way down her thighs with some Christian Louboutin Pigalle 120 Strass-Gold Pumps. Rosalina knew them at first sight because her and her home girls were just online looking at them. They were three thousand dollars out the door! She couldn't afford to spend that much money on a pair of shoes. Terrance wasn't paying her that well and Quick Money cheap Crab ass damn sure wouldn't buy them for her.

Lisa walked up and spoke to Rosalina. "Sorry I am a late sweetheart. I had some last-minute business to finish up."

"No problem Lisa. I was on Instagram posting pictures from the HB Murda concert killing time," said Rosalina. "You look good Boss Lady."

"Thank you, Rosalina. That's so sweet of you."

"Just saying you're bad that's all," said Rosalina with a smile on her face. "I love your shoes. Me and my girls were just online looking at them last night."

"These old things? Terrance bought them as a gift for me on my birthday."

"Damn Boss Lady you and Terrance are really close huh? How does his girl feel about that?"

"Me and Kay are very cool. She knows Terrance is my brother and nothing more."

"I don't know if I could be that trusting."

"It's called growing up Rosalina. Now let's go get our table. I am starving."

Lisa got the first response she was wanting from Rosalina. Now it was time to milk the cow at the dinner table and find out what Rosalina's real angle was.

After dinner and a bottle of champagne, Rosalina was feeling good. Lisa knew it was the right time to go in for the kill. "So, are you dating anyone right now?" Lisa asked.

Rosalina hesitated and then said, "Yes, if you want to call it that. I think I am just another one of his sliders. He only calls me for sex and information about..." Rosalina caught herself before it slipped out of her mouth, but Lisa already was on point. She just let it slide like she didn't hear anything but she definitely took down the mental side note.

"Boss Lady, I really enjoyed this dinner meeting. I want to have money and power like you one day," said Rosalina. "I love the fact that you are a very strong and independent woman."

Lisa felt sorry for Rosalina. She knew her struggle. They both grew up without a stable home, Lisa was just lucky enough to have Terrance. He was always there for her so she didn't have to deal with the extra trauma that young girls go through growing up.

"So, where did your home girls go after the concert?" asked Lisa.

"I don't know, I think they said they were trying to get in the after-party," said Rosalina.

"Cool. Call them up and tell them to meet us there. I have a fifteen seat VIP section by the Deejay booth."

"For real Boss Lady? Oh my God, I love you!" said Rosalina.

*   *   *

The line was wrapped around the corner. This was the official after-party for the concert. Everybody that was anybody in the city was there for this event. Lisa pulled up to the valet and hopped out like the boss bitch that she was. Everybody important knew who Lisa was; her name carried weight in every state. Rosalina was enjoying every second of this. She never moved around the city in this fashion. They walked right past the line, straight in the door and past the security check.

Rosalina's girlfriends were all dime pieces. They were also all thots. Tonight, was different. Tonight, they would be the ones being watched. Their section was in the middle of BiM Mathis and HB Murda sections. No doubt, the best spot in the room. The professional ball players weren't even allowed in this prime real estate unless they were with RocNation. Lisa ordered ten bottles of Ace of Spade, two bottles of D'usse, four bottles of Cîroc and a bottle of Hennessy just in case Pistol Pete decided to come through. It was always family first. They called Pistol Pete, Tee, and Lisa the three amigos. When the bottles arrived, the sparkles lit up the whole damn club. The Deejay shouted out Lisa and HB Murda saluted her. This was a typical night out on the town for Lisa. Terrance always taught her not to do anything halfway. Squad Boy TV was filming the whole club event tonight. It was like a real-life movie scene. Plus, all this was for a small part of

Lisa's plan. She needed to "WOW" Rosalina and gain all of her trust.

Quick Money was in the club on the floor level. They had the section next to the bar. All of the sparkles from Lisa bottles caught his attention. When DJ Mike P mentioned Lisa and Camp5 in the building "Going Up," that's when Quick Money noticed Rosalina standing next to Lisa. He instantly got pissed off at her.

Quick Money was looking so crazy, Fox noticed and asked him "Everything good?"

All Quick Money could see was Lisa's diamonds dancing. He wanted nothing else but to rape, rob and throw that bitch off the bridge buck naked. You could see the envy in his eyes. He looked like a possessed man.

Lisa knew the enemy was out there somewhere watching. She knew Rosalina was her bait. If someone was using Rosalina to get inside of Camp5's organization they would show their face tonight for sure.

The night continued on without any problems. Lisa was not drinking heavily anymore. She needed to focus and stay on point so she was sipping light. The other girls were turning up enjoying the limelight. Rosalina reached over to Lisa and kissed her on the neck and said, "Thanks Boss Lady for a wonderful night. I have to go to the restroom and I will be right back." She and two other girls got up and walked down the stairs to the VIP bathroom. Lisa pointed at one of her undercover bodyguards and told them to follow them from behind to make sure they were ok. Lisa knew if someone was watching them this would be the perfect time for them to make their move on Rosalina when they thought that she would be most vulnerable and alone.

Ten minutes later Rosalina came out of the restroom. Quick Money grabbed her by the arm. "Rosa what the fuck you doing here with that sour bitch?" asked Quick Money.

Before Rosalina could answer, Lisa came out of nowhere and asked Quick Money, "Who are you calling a sour a bitch? Pussy ass fuck boy!" Quick Money saw Lisa and tried to charge her. Before he could take two steps, two huge guards grabbed him up and choked him out the club's back door. Quick Money was raising so much hell that the club owner trespassed him and banned him from the club. The police escorted Quick Money off the premises to the car and demanded he leave or go to jail.

*　　　*　　　*

Terrance was sitting in his office at home thinking about his showcases. First on the agenda was New York, he knew there would be a lot of big spenders in town during fashion week. Los Angeles was more like a show and tell. Everybody out there was looking for the free shit. They just wanted a sponsor so they could look good wearing your jewels, to all of the big movie premieres, so the blogs could talk about what they were wearing and how it looked. The ones that did buy spent millions of dollars on jewelry, the price never mattered. They always made their purchases on the spot. Atlanta would be the third stop. The Dirty South always showed their support and love for Camp5 no matter if it was in the music business, fashion world, or the jewelry game, they always came out in multitudes. Miami would be the last stop of the tour. The bottom of the map is MI yay-yo, the city that the cocaine cowboys built. This one had to be the big finale. Terrance had a lot of big things planned. His first agenda would be the big marriage proposal to Kay that he managed to keep secret from everyone. He had already arranged for her family and his family to be in Miami for a week-long engagement cruise. Right after the showcase, they would all leave Sunday night for the Virgin Islands.

The hardest thing was going to be going straight and leaving his brothers in the game. Because they had been side by side in the trenches for so long, it didn't feel right getting out. Terrance knew it was time for an exit. No one retired from the dope game—either you quit, or the game took you out, death or prison. Blaze was a prime example of the prison theory and Jamaican Wayne was the ugly truth of what could happen if you get caught slipping. Terrance was wondering what happened to Mr. Wayne. He was a good dude; he couldn't understand why someone would want to take him out. The game was fucked up and that's why it was time for him to get out. All of Terrance's thoughts had him exhausted. He cut the power off his laptop and went upstairs and got in the bed with Kay.

*   *   *

The time was getting late. Lisa was ready to leave the club. She had already found out everything she thought she needed to know about Rosalina. Lisa told Rosalina she was on her way out and asked if she was going to catch one of her home girls' home or get an Uber? Rosalina said, "No Boss Lady, I came with you, I am leaving with you." Lisa and Rosalina walk out of the club. The valet had already pulled her car around. She tipped him a hundred dollars, jumped in and pulled off... Rosalina asked Lisa to take her to a hotel because she was afraid the guy might be waiting on her at her apartment.

Lisa said, "You don't need to go through all that baby girl. I have a three-bedroom condo. You can crash there tonight."

Rosa got emotional and started crying. "Thanks Lisa. You don't have to be so kind to me. Thank you so much."

Lisa grabbed her hand. She couldn't stand to see this lost little girl crying and in so much pain.

Quick Money was sitting on Rosalina's couch mad as fuck looking at his knock off Gucci watch that he purchased from the flea market and flipping through channels talking to himself. Rosalina knew Quick Money would go to her house because she gave him a key. Plus... he had been texting her crazy message ever since he got kicked out the club. Quick Money knew he fucked up by blowing a lid like that, but that high yellow bitch surprised him coming out of nowhere with her slick ass mouth. Someone needs to put that uppity bitch in her place. Quick Money figured he was the one to do it. First, he needed to know what Rosalina was even doing with this bitch anyways. He heard in the streets that Lisa liked girls but no one ever came up with the solid proof. Never mind that. First thing in the morning he was going to talk to Lucky Lefty. They needed to make their move on Camp5 now not later!

Lisa pulled up to the gated community and pressed a button for the gates to open. Armed security was everywhere. The waterfalls were beautiful against the town home signs. Rosalina didn't even know this place existed. She was blown away by the town homes. She knew Lisa had to be spending a lot of money to live here. Lisa pulled into her two-car garage right beside her Range Rover.

Rosalina said, "I hope I am not interrupting anything Boss Lady."

Lisa asked Rosalina what she meant by that.

"I thought your man may be here. I see the truck in the garage."

"No baby, no man is in here. These are both of my cars. Come on, let me show you to your sleeping quarters for tonight. The towels and everything else you need are in the cabinets. You can use the bathrobe on the door. I will get you a t-shirt and some shorts to sleep in.

After a thirty-minute bath Rosalina got out of the tub feeling much better. She only has a shower at her apartment. Rosalina was thinking how much she needed that bubble bath. Her shorts and shirt were laying on the bed. She smelled some breakfast cooking, so she went into the kitchen.

Lisa said, "Girl I was hungry as hell. I cooked enough for you, if you want some."

Lisa house was laid out; it was decorated so nice that Rosalina was afraid to touch anything. As they were sitting down eating and watching TV, Lisa could feel Rosalina's eyes watching her. She looked up to see if she was looking at her. For sure, she was looking...

Lisa smiled and asked Rosalina what was wrong. Rosalina said "Boss Lady, I think you are fine ass fuck. I want to taste you. I hope I am not violating you."

Lisa grabbed Rosalina's head and pushed it down in between her legs. Rosalina started tasting her. She said, "Now you are violating me. Keep violating me just like that."

Lisa hadn't been with a girl since her first year in college. Rosalina was a bad little baby that had never been with a girl. And since Terrance couldn't have her, she figured she might as well be her first experience with a woman. Lisa walked Rosalina to her master bedroom. Laid her down on the bed and took out all of her toys. They played sex games until the sun came up. Rosalina had never felt this good in all of her experiences with sex. Her head was spinning; she was all messed up. Before she knew it, she was fast asleep like a baby.

Chapter 17

Jackie was getting dressed for her dinner date with US Marshal Tommy. This was more business than pleasure. She needed to know how much the US Government had on Kenny and his crew. They arrived at this Cuban restaurant downtown. It had the best beans and rice in town and the steak was great. Everyone that worked there was Spanish so the food was authentic. The two sat down at their table. Tommy was excited to be spending time with his old flame. Jackie was nervous because once again she was in too deep.

"So how do you really like the south?" Tommy asked Jackie.

"It's a great place. Just hot as hell down here. Totally different heat then Arizona and Mexico. A lot of humidity, but I love the beaches. The water is so beautiful," Jackie told Tommy.

"I know after things went down with the Cartel you needed a break but I never thought that you would leave the Bureau. What happened?"

"After I recovered from the injuries, my director told me I needed to retire because of the physical and emotional trauma I went through. They gave me all of my benefits with a full pension. I figured that since I always love the calmness of water, why not come to Florida. It's the place where all the retired people come, right? Somehow, I ended up in this small county. bored with nothing to do so I decide to get back into law enforcement. That's how I ended up working in classifications. I also have a family member that lives here.

So why did Captain Rogers call in the heavy hitters? I didn't realize we had that much going on in Highlands County?"

"Listen Jackie. The department knows that someone on the inside is helping Kenny and his crew. They want to nail them to the wall just as much as they want to get Kenny Thomas. So, whoever the moles are... I feel sorry for them. Captain Rogers is on a mission to clean up his department and wipe out all of the corrupt officers," said Douglas.

Jackie knew her next move had to be well planned out. The department was too small. If they started snooping around in the right places, she was bound to be discovered as the mole. Jackie needed a scapegoat, someone to switch the heat to before it got too close to her. She knew Slim's murder would be charged to the corrupt officers involved. Murdering a federal informant was the death penalty for sure. Agent Tommy noticed the look of discomfort on Jackie's face and decided to switch the topic of conversation.

"Enough about work. So why don't you have any kids or a husband yet?"

Jackie just wasn't the type of woman that wanted to settle down and be a housewife. Taking care of kids and a husband was not for her. She lived for the thrill and danger.

"Why aren't you married yet?' Jackie replied. "I would think by now you would be all settled down with kids and a beautiful wife."

"Actually, I am married. We have two kids together, a three-year-old girl and a one-year-old boy.

"So, who is the lucky lady?" Jackie asked.

"Agent Campbell," replied Tommy.

"My former work colleague?"

He nodded.

"Son of a bitch I knew she had the hots for you that's why that heifer never liked me. Always making smart remarks and breathing down my neck! So how did this happen exactly? And don't spare any details."

"Well... when you went undercover with your last assignment. I was under so much stress and she was there for me. It started out as drinking partners, just blowing off work-related steam."

"Yeah, I bet that wasn't the only thing you two were letting off!" said Jackie.

"Jackie, you can't be bitter about this. You left me for the job. What did you expect, for me to wait around forever?"

"No, I expected for you to be loyal and not go and fucking marry my co-worker." Jackie jumped up and stormed away from the table and out of the restaurant. Tommy left one hundred and fifty dollars on the table and ran out of the restaurant behind Jackie. Tommy loved his wife, but Jackie would always have a place in his heart. He was reminded of that when he saw her back at the Sheriff's Office.

"Wait Jackie, let me explain."

"There is nothing to explain Tommy."

Jackie tipped the valet driver, jumped in her car and pulled off.

Jackie was pissed off about Tommy and Agent Campbell, but she knew that she had to get her head back in the game fast if she was to survive this mess that her and Kenny were in. Detective Jones was sitting at home when his phone rang from an anonymous number. It was early Sunday morning. The guy on the line asked for a meeting today at three o'clock pm. Detective Jones agreed and hung up the phone. His phone rang again. This time it was the sexy officer, Jackie Diaz. She seemed upset about something. Worried about her, he asked if everything was alright and if she needed anything from him.

She replied, "only your company." Detective Jones got dressed and headed over to meet with Jackie at her apartment. He was surprised when she opened the door still in her nightgown. Detective Jones couldn't believe that he was finally getting lucky.

"Come inside handsome. Are you just going to stand there with your mouth open, or do what you've been wanting to do to me for the last ten months?" asked Jackie. Detective Jones grabbed Jackie and slammed her against the couch and began ripping his clothes off, thinking in his head that he wasn't moving fast enough. So, he just pulled it out through his zipper and pressed it on her. Jackie moaned with pleasure. Detective Jones was like a wild animal; she couldn't believe how good this actually was. Jackie needed to release some stress and she needed to figure out a way to set Detective Jones up to take the fall for being the mole inside the department. She knew taking it to the sex level with Detective Jones would blind him of her plan that she had been putting in motion ever since she stormed off from the dinner with U.S. Marshal Douglas. Jackie was a rattlesnake. One of the worst kinds because she didn't have any rattlers to warn you that you were in danger whenever you were getting in bed with her.

Detective Jones looked at his phone. It was around two o'clock. He knew he had an important meeting in an hour, so he told Jackie he had to go and see his mom. Something about taking her grocery shopping. She knew that was bullshit because she had been watching Jones while he was checking his text messages. Jackie was so good that she remembered the address and the meeting time, three o'clock.

Detective Jones pulled up to the lake and got into an all-black dodge challenger. Jackie had been trailing him the whole way from her house. She needed solid evidence that Jones was crooked and this was the only way she could get her plan to work. Jackie was snapping pictures; she couldn't ID the driver, but she had plenty of pictures of Detective Jones getting in and out of the suspect's car. When Detective Jones sat down in the challenger and shut the door, Terrance asked him what's up with the tail that he brought with him?

Jones was lost for words he had no idea that someone was following him. "Come on brother, you are getting sloppy. What's clouding your mind today?" asked Terrance.

"Nothing." But the whole ride over he was thinking about that good hole Jackie Diaz had between her legs. Terrance saved Jones' life when they were kids. Kenny tried to kill him about a girl and Terrance jumped in front of the gun. The bullet hit Terrance in the arm. It only left him with some minor flesh lacerations but nothing too serious. At the hospital, they all lied and told the police that a black car with tinted windows did a drive-by. After that Terrance and Jones always remained close friends. Jones never liked Kenny; he couldn't wait to give that bastard a life sentence.

Terrance needed to talk to Detective Jones about doing armed security for his upcoming showcases. He needed someone that he could trust on the ground that he knew would always run a tight ship. Detective Jones had done a lot of off duty security work for Terrance back in the day when he was still promoting concerts and other lavish events.

This was a great opportunity for everyone to make a good amount of cash, so he decided to give everyone a slice of the pie. This was just the type of guy that Terrance was. Detective Jones told Terrance he couldn't get away right now to do it because of the heavy workload at the Sheriff's Office. He recommended him to another security firm. He also mentions to Terrance that the DEA was asking questions and throwing his name around in a meeting early last week, Tee told Jones that he appreciated the information and would look into it. Detective Jones got out of the black challenger and opened the door to his gray impala sedan. He looked into his rearview mirror and couldn't find the tail Terrance had just warned him about.

*   *   *

Pistol Pete was sitting at the bar around noon having a drink and talking to a stripper named Destiny. Feeling down and out because his main man Terrance was getting out of the game and he knew there was nothing he could do to change his mind. Once Terrance made his mind up that was final. No one could persuade him to do anything different than what he was thinking. Destiny was so fine that any other day Pete would be throwing money her way and turning up. She knew he was down and cheering him up was a part of her job. Destiny grabbed Pete's hand and walked him over to the private dance room. He was feeling down and out of it, but never too down for some good pussy and head in the champagne room. As Pistol Pete was walking into the private room with Destiny, Quick Money was walking in through the front door. As soon as he spotted Pete, Quick Money started reaching for his gun. "Fuck," said Quick Money. He was empty-handed. There were no weapons allowed in Tootsie's and the day shift was the worst. They were extra strict on the weapons policy.

Quick Money's brain started racing. This was the perfect time to take Terrance's right-hand man out of the picture. Pistol Pete was alone and vulnerable, plus he was unaware that Quick was even there plotting on him. Quick Money purchased a double shot of Hennessy from the bartender and killed it in one swallow. After that he made his way outside to his car to wait for Pistol Pete to leave the club.

Adrian was calling Pistol Pete, but Pistol was not answering his phone. They were supposed to meet up at Tootsies for some drinks. Pistol Pete told Adrian that he had a lot on his mind and needed to talk to him about it. Destiny made Pete's day feel a little better after giving him what every man that paid their admission at Tootsie's fantasize about. That was taking her fine ass for a sexual ride. Pistol Pete looked down at his cellphone damn he had five missed phone calls. Just that fast Pete had forgotten Adrian was supposed to be meeting him for some drinks and conversation. It was always crazy how a good head doctor and great cookies will make you lose track of the time...every time. Pistol Pete stepped outside to smoke a cigarette, and called Adrian back. As he was reaching for his lighter, he heard gunshots.

Chapter 18

Black Boy jumped out his car looking over his shoulders trying to make sure that Fred and the Muck Boyz didn't follow him to meet up with Jamaican key-Tee. When Key-Tee saw the look on Black Boy's face, he knew something was terribly wrong.

"Wan go on King? Look like you saw a ghost, my boy?"

"Look Key-Tee I am going to be straight up with you. Me and you have been dealing for too long of a time for me to try and bullshit you or not be straight forward. Yesterday some guys from down south called the Muck Boyz ran down on me with semi-automatics and forced me in the truck with them. They were asking questions about you and the operation. They gave me no options. It was given you up or watch my baby mother and kid die before they killed me. No one threatens my baby's life. Fuck that and them I am ready to die today. Just say the word."

Key-Tee told Black Boy, "Just chill my youth. The boy them you fa talked about killed Jamaican Wayne the other night. I knew they ran down on you. I just wanted to see how loyal you were to me. I got some shooters watching your family right now, King."

Black Boy was relieved and for a good reason. If he had not told Key-Tee the truth, chances are that would have been his last conversation and the shooters that were watching his family would have been killing his family. Key-Tee was just as ruthless as the Muck Boyz with a track record long enough to prove it.

"Listen King this is what we fa do. Go back and give them all the information that they are looking fa and when the time is right, we will throw them a welcome party!"

Freddy and Juan were sitting in the car watching Black Boy baby mother's house, when a call came in that it was Black Boy asking them to meet him in an hour at the carwash on Hal McRae Blvd. Freddy was very anxious to meet with Black Boy. This was his first chance to find out some real solid information on the guy who killed his cousin Slim. Freddy and Juan pulled into the carwash in the black Tahoe. Willie, Walter and Ralph were parked across the street, just in case, this was a set up. They were ready for anything to happen at this point.

Black Boy jumped into the Tahoe with Freddy and Juan. "What's up gangsters? I have some valuable information for you today. I met with Key-tee last night. He has a big deal going down in a few weeks. I figured we can both come out of this deal with something to gain. You get to kill him and I get to take over his turf."

Freddy smiled at Black Boy and said, "I like the way you think. So where is this deal going down at"

"All I know right now is his warehouse out on Highway 64. I am still working on all of the details."

96

"Ok good work Black! Make sure you stay on top of this. We need to throw this pussy clot a Jamaican surprise birthday party real soon."

"Bet," said Black Boy as he jumped out of the Tahoe. He was anxious to tell Key-tee that Freddy and his crew were buying his story.

Juan looked at Freddy and told him, "Brother, it's something I don't like about that puta. I can feel it in my bones."

Freddy said, "Don't worry my brother. We are going to put that puta in the same hole that we put his boss in. As soon as we get all the information that we need from him, his time and value will be expiring real soon."

* * *

Pistol Pete tried to run for cover, but it was nowhere to go. The shots from Quick Money gun were coming out so fast it seemed like three people were shooting at him. Adrian heard the gunshots when he was pulling off the highway into Tootsie's parking lot. It sounded like someone was letting off firecrackers. Immediately, Adrian reached for his pistol, just in case he needed to use it. Pistol Pete was laying in the doorway of the club bleeding out like a wild hog in the broad daylight. Quick Money jumped in his car and pulled out of the parking lot. Adrian looked right in his face as he was pulling into the parking lot. Adrian could feel something was not right. It's like he knew what had happened to Pistol Pete just by the look on Quick Money's face! Adrian jumped out of the car. He could see some people standing at the entrance of the club standing over a body. Destiny was screaming and crying so loud, telling Pete to breathe. The security guard was on the phone calling 911.

Adrian ran up to Pistol Pete, picked him up and started dragging his lifeless body to the car. Pistol Pete was barely conscious. Adrian was telling Pete "Breathe, just breathe! You are going to make it brother... just breathe!"

Terrance walked in the living room from the kitchen and heard his cell phone vibrating on the couch. When Terrance tried to grab the phone, it was too late. He had already missed the call. Before he had a chance to call Adrian, Kay came downstairs yelling and crying!

"Pete just got shot, somebody shot Pete!"

"Kay calm down baby and tell me what happened."

"Terrance! Somebody just shot my brother! I can't be calm!" Kay said. Crying out of control.

The phone rang again. It was Adrian. "Pistol at the Florida Hospital and it's not looking good. You need to get here fast!"

Terrance grabbed his keys. Him and Kay jumped in and pulled off burning rubber.

Chapter 19

Lucky Lefty got a text from Quick Money with the code numbers 603911. That code meant drop everything and meet me at the spot. Lucky Lefty called Tracy and asked her to put his food in the microwave because he knew this was going to be a long night. The last time Lucky had seen this code, Quick Money had been shot and robbed for two bricks. Right now, in this moment and time, the Down 4 Myne Crew couldn't stand a loss so big. Riding down 27 all Terrance could see was his homie, Pistol Pete face, and the only thing Terrance could think about was the last conversation he had with Pete earlier that week...

Terrance told Pete that he was finished with the dope game after this load and that it was time for them all to get out. Pistol Pete wasn't too happy about the news. Terrance couldn't help but wonder if that was going to be his last conversation that he ever had with his brother.

Terrance and Kay pulled up to the Florida Hospital at the emergency room entrance. Everyone was standing outside. Some people were crying, some people were praying and others were crying and praying. The Camp5 Crew was huddled up in a circle talking privately. Everyone stopped talking and got quiet when Terrance walked up. Adrian's clothes were covered in Pistol Pete's blood. As calmly as possible, Terrance asked, "Adrian what the fuck happened out there today?"

"Terrance when I was pulling up to meet Pistol at Tootsies. I heard shots being fired. As I am coming into the parking lot, I see Quick Money pulling out of the parking lot. He was not in a hurry. He was just pulling out normal," said Adrian. "Pussy looked me right in my face! I know he did this shit!" Adrian was so loud that people started staring at them.

"Calm down bruh. We got eyes on us," Jamal told Adrian. Everyone was trying to keep their composure. This was a very emotional time. Their brother was in the emergency room fighting for his life.

"Listen, I am going to go back in here with Kay and her parents. Tonya is dropping their kids off to Grandma Joanna and then she will be on her way."

"That's a totally different beast," said Jason.

"Yeah, I know," replied Terrance. "Let's all just try and get through the night. We will meet up and work out the details in the morning at the honeycomb hideout," said Terrance.

Lucky Lefty pulled up to the spot to meet up with Quick Money, but there were no cars parked out front or on the side of the house. Lucky figured Quick Money had to be parked in the back, so no one would notice that he was there. Lucky Lefty was thinking to himself this had to be a serious matter because Quick Money never parked in the back. Lucky Lefty walked downstairs to the basement. Quick Money was sitting in a chair smoking a cigarette, drinking some liquor and playing with his gun at the same time.

"What's wrong?" asked Lucky Lefty.

"Man Luck, I had to burn that nigga," said Quick Money.

"Hold up. Burn what nigga?"

"That bitch ass nigga Pistol Pete!" said Quick Money.

"Nigga is you crazy! We are not ready to go to war with them Camp5 niggas! And then you touch Terrance right-hand man! Nigga is you snorting that shit again?" asked Lucky Lefty. Quick Money was a fool, but he wasn't a damn fool. He knew Lucky Lefty was very nice with his hands and he also knew Lucky was always ready to get on that gunplay.

Anyways Lucky was dead ass right about him using it again. Ever since he saw that bitch Lisa in the club with his chick Rosalina, Quick Money hadn't been able to get his thoughts together.

"Listen Quick, just lay low for right now. The streets are already way too hot and too many bodies have been dropping around here lately," said Lucky Lefty. "Give me a few days to sort this shit out okay!"

Quick Money apologized to Lucky for his stupidity and told him that it would never happen again. Lucky felt bad for his best friend. He knew Quick Money was really going through some things right now and all he wanted to do was be there for him.

Chapter 20

The Sheriff's Office phones were ringing off the hook about a club shooting. Everyone was scrambling trying to get into their patrol cars and rush to the scene of the crime. Detective Jones and Detective Smith arrived at the crime scene together in an unmarked car. It looked like a war zone in the parking lot. U.S. Marshal Tommy called Detective Smith and told him that it wasn't looking good for the shooting victim and he didn't think that Peter Walker aka Pistol Pete was going to make it through the night.

Detective Smith relayed the message to Detective Jones. First thing that came to Jones' mind was Terrance. He knew how close Terrance and Peter were; they all grew up together in the same neighborhood off of Washington Street. After processing the scene, Detective Smith and Jones left for the Florida Hospital. The place was packed and people were everywhere. Detective Jones greeted the Walker family with his condolence, gave Kay and Tonya a hug, then asked Terrance to step off and talk to him in private.

"Look Tee. I know you and Pete are like brothers, but let us do our jobs. I promise you we are going to get the son of a bitch that did this to Peter," said Detective Jones.

Terrance looked Detective Jones right in his eyes and stated, "I have no doubt that you will do your job. Now can I get back to my family Detective?"

"Yes, you may, but remember what I said."

*   *   *

Lucky Lefty pulled up in his yard. The whole way there he was trying to come up with a strategy. Quick Money had jumped the fucking gun. He had let his pride and emotions get the best of him now the whole plan had been jeopardized. Lucky Lefty knew Terrance would not stop at any cost to find out who shot his right-hand man. He was practically married to Pistol Pete's sister. They were like brothers. Lucky knew what this was going to lead to once the Camp5 Crew found out Quick Money was behind the shooting; it was time to call in for reinforcement that was the only way to survive this situation.

*   *   *

Rosalina had been hanging out at Lisa's house the last few days, laying low trying to let Quick Money cool off. Quick Money had tried to reach out to her a couple of times, leaving voicemails apologizing about the incident at the club, but she never responded to him. Lisa got the call from Jason that Pistol Pete had been shot and the outcome wasn't looking too good. He told her to get to the Florida Hospital ASAP! Rosalina overheard the conversation and asked Lisa if she could drop her off home on her way to the Florida Hospital? Rosalina needed to get some clothes and also check on her apartment. She had not been back there since the club incident.

The apartment was dark and cold when Rosalina unlocked the door and walked in. She walked to the living room wall and turned on all the lights and was surprised to see Quick Money laying on her couch.

"Babe, Babe, are you alright?"

Quick Money jumped up like he had seen a ghost, paranoid and holding his pistol. "Rosie, don't scare me like that! You almost just got shot, woman!"

"Why are you still at my house?"

"Why are you just getting home? And not answering any of my messages?"

Rosalina said, "I asked you my question first."

Quick Money said, "I don't give a fuck what you ask me. Answer my question before I—"

"Before you what?" asked Rosalina with confidence in her voice.

Lisa was almost two city blocks away from Rosalina house when she heard a phone vibrating in-between the passenger seat of her car. When she reached down and got it, she saw that it was Rosalina's cell phone. She decides to turn around and take Rosalina's phone back to her. With all the stuff that was going on with Pete, it wasn't any telling when she would be free to see Rosalina again.

By now Quick Money was mad all over again. Talking loudly and cursing Rosalina out. Asking where she had been for the last few days. He grabbed her around the neck and asked her what she was doing in the club with that bitch Lisa.

Lisa was just about to ring the doorbell when she heard a commotion going on inside of Rosalina apartment. She knew the male voice was punk-ass Quick Money. Quick Money, overcome with emotion, told Rosalina, "I am going to kill that bitch Lisa next. The same way I ran down on her homeboy Pistol Pete today. Fuck Camp5! All of them niggas are going to die and you are going to continue to help me and Lucky set it up!" said Quick Money.

Before Rosalina had a chance to respond, the doorbell rang. Quick Money in such a rage, not thinking who it might be, opened the door, and screamed out "WHAT?"

Lisa had her Colt 45 in Quick Money's face. Shocked to see Lisa, Quick Money stood in the doorway emotionless.

"Pussy nigga, this what!" Screamed Lisa, pulling the trigger. Then again. And again.

Quick Money's lifeless body drops to the floor. Lisa then turned the gun on a screaming and frightened Rosalina. "Pussy hoe, you were trying to set me and my brothers up?"

"No, I can explain!" said Rosalina.

"Too late bitch!" said Lisa and fired again, then twice more. Rosalina's body dropped to the floor.

James' burner phone was vibrating. The text came from Lisa's burner phone with a simple message that read, "I need a cleaning crew at 603 Fred O'Conner,

Street ASAP." Without ever needing to respond to Lisa's text, James sent a crew in to clean up the job.

Chapter 21

Freddy and his crew were sitting at the local bar, called Club Cino's. Grabbing a bite to eat and washing it down with a few drinks. When Black Boy called him wanting to meet up around eight-thirty to talk about Key Tee and the warehouse deal that was going down. Freddy was excited to finally meet the mutherfucka that put his cousin Slim to sleep and to repay him the favor. The plan had already been set in motion. Black Boy and Key-Tee were prepared to give the Muck Boyz a party of a lifetime.

Juan was soaking up all of the information that Black Boy was providing them with about Key-Tee detail for details. Something just didn't feel right. The layout was too sweet to be true. If Key-Tee was this easy to touch, why hasn't anyone killed this fool? Juan asked himself. Freddy was so caught up in getting revenge that he was not thinking logically. Set up or not, Freddy wanted Key-Tee dead and his mind was set on being the one to do it! When the Muck Boyz pulled up to the warehouse, the set up was perfect everything was in play just like Black Boy said it would be. Key-Tee was sitting down in the warehouse office when he saw the black Tahoe pull up to the back of the building. He knew what time it was. Everybody was in place to welcome Freddy and the Muck Boyz.

As Freddy was about to get out of the truck and go into the warehouse with his guns blazing, his cell phone started ringing. "Fuck," said Freddy. "It's Terrance." He didn't want to answer but he knew if Tee was calling, this shit had to be important, so Freddy answered.

"Yo Freddy, I need you ASAP! Somebody just shot Pistol Pete and it is not looking good."

"Ok where are you at?"

"The Florida Hospital in Sebring," said Terrance.

"Ok, I will be there in thirty minutes."

Terrance paused for a moment after he hung up the phone with Freddy and asked himself how could Freddy get from the Muck to the Florida Hospital so fast? That was at least an hour and a half away even if he were speeding.

Freddy hung up the phone and told Juan, rain check. We got to get this fool on the rebound. Our brothers need us right now."

"What happened?" Juan asked Freddy.

"Pistol Pete just got shot and it's not looking too good," Freddy responded.

To be honest Juan was relieved because he didn't feel good about running into that warehouse. For one he didn't trust Black Boy's word and for two something just smelled really fishy about it!

The black Tahoe was backing out of the warehouse. Key-Tee and Black Boy were watching them on the camera's trying to figure out what was going on. Maybe they saw something that tipped them off. Maybe they figured out Black Boy was playing them or just maybe they didn't want to die tonight. Whatever the reason was for them leaving, Key-Tee was not going to give them another shot at him. From this point on, he was about to be the aggressor.

Chapter 22

By the time Lisa arrived at the Florida Hospital, things had already calmed down and everyone was just sitting and waiting around for some type of good news. She walked up to Pistol's Pete family and gave all of them a hug and a few words of encouragement, before asking Terrance to come outside and take a walk with her. Lisa and Terrance stepped outside the emergency room sliding doors. Lisa was so hot that she could barely keep her composure.

"I shot that nigga and his pussy ass hoe!" said Lisa

"What? Slow down Lisa," said Terrance. "You shot what nigga and what hoe?"

"That nigga Quick Money and that flaw ass bitch you had working for us, Rosalina."

"Wait, why would you do that?" said Terrance.

"Basically, Lucky Lefty and the Down 4 Myne Crew placed that bitch on the inside to infiltrate us and find out all the information on us that she could so that they could try and take us out. The other night I took her out to dinner. Then I took her and her thot ass friends out to the club after the HB Murda and BiM Mathis concert to get her to try and loosen up around me so I could get some information out of her. Anyways she left the "VIP" table to use the ladies room. That's when this nigga Quick Money ran down on her as she was leaving out of the ladies room.

I had to intervene and had that nigga kicked out of the club! I should have known something then, the way he was cursing me out and trying to get to me!"

"Damn Lisa you were supposed to call me right then!" said Terrance.

"I didn't have enough to go on at the time. It was still all just speculations."

"I can understand that," said Terrance. He knew Lisa was a bloodhound for information because he trained her to be. "So, when and why did you shoot them?"

"On my way over here," Lisa answered Terrance. "I was dropping that bitch off at home on the way here... another long story. I realized two blocks away from her house that she had left her phone in my car. So, I turned around to take it to her. When I got to the door, I heard a male voice yelling. Immediately I recognized Quick Money's voice from the club the other night. I heard him admit to shooting Pistol Pete and also saying he was going to kill me. He then continues to say that she was going to continue to get information to set you up for him and Lucky Lefty. So, I rang the doorbell and shot both of them in the face. James got the cleaning crew over there right now cleaning that shit up."

Terrance started rubbing his head he could not believe that this nigga Kenny was plotting to take him out. Especially after he had let him live last time.

It was time to checkmate this sucker; no more excuses. Lucky Lefty hand drew first blood and now it was time for him to go. "Okay Lisa you know the drill go and burn everything and wait for me at my house. Freddy is on his way up here," said Terrance.

"Freddy?" asked Lisa. She knew what Freddy coming up here meant. It was never good news for anyone when Freddy was coming to town. Unless someone was getting married or it was a funeral. Lisa didn't want to leave without seeing Pistol Pete, but she knew she had to go and get rid of all the evidence of the double homicide she had just committed.

*   *   *

Lucky Lefty called Quick Money five times in a row. The only thing he was getting was the voicemail. Something in his stomach just didn't feel right. He knew something was wrong. Ten minutes later, a phone call came in from Fox.

"Lucky, get to the trap now. They just found Quick Money and some Spanish chick dead in her apartment. I think someone tried to rob them; they got the whole complex roped off with yellow tape!" said Fox.

Lucky knew what time it was. Quick Money and Rosalina's plan had been exposed. Terrance and his Camp5 Crew would be looking for him next. It was time to make his next move. Detective Jones and Detective Smith got a call from the homicide division. They were told that they were needed at a double murder scene, over in the Tangelo Park area. *Tonight, was too damn young to be this busy.* Detective Jones thought to himself. All of these recent fatal shootings had to be connected somehow. When the detective's walked in the apartment, the first thing they recognized was how professional this hit was. The only evidence left behind were the two dead corpses. The dead male was identified as Jacob Massey alias Quick Money, better known as Kenny Thomas', aka Lucky Lefty, right hand man. Lieutenant and the next in line to run the Down 4 Myne Crew. The female victim was Rosalina Rodriguez. She was a stunning beauty! Detective Jones was shaking his head thinking of how that was such a good waste of a young lady and probably some good cut up, gone way too soon.

Lucky Lefty was crying sitting in his car, bumping Tupac's song *How Long Will They Mourn Me,* with his pistol sitting on his lap. Quick Money was the closest thing to a brother Lucky Lefty had since his real brother Spider caught life in prison, when he was sixteen. The only thing Lucky could think about was Quick Money's smile and the corny ass jokes that he told. No matter what, Terrance and his Camp5 Crew were going to pay for this with their lives—every last one of them.

Chapter 23

Freddy pulled up to Florida Hospital and texted Terrance to come outside. There were too many police cars for him to come inside. When Terrance got outside to the truck, he jumped in the back seat with Freddy and began to explain to him and Juan exactly what was going on. Freddy and Juan just sat back and listened carefully, taking it all in.

When Terrance finished. In the calmest voice possible, Freddy asked Terrance, "So what are you going to do about it?"

Terrance's response was simple. "I am going to send this nigga to hell, for good!"

"Now you're talking, brother," said Juan. He was always ready for that type of action. After thirty minutes of conversation and plotting on Lucky Lefty and his crew, Freddy's phone started ringing. Freddy said out loud, "Damn. It's that fuck nigga Black Boy." Juan told him not to answer and just leave that fuck nigga guessing.

Terrance usually didn't get into other people's business, but he just had to know what business Freddy and Muck Boyz had going on with Black Boy. Terrance knew that nigga Black Boy was a creep and really bad for business. Freddy asked Terrance if he remembered his first cousin Slim from Belle-glade?

"Yeah," responded Terrance. "He was cool as hell. I just couldn't rock with him because of the company that he was always around. He was affiliated with the Down 4 Myne Crew, right?"

"Yes, that's him. I tried to tell him that the fools were bad news and that they didn't mean him no good and to come back home. But my cousin would not listen to me," said Freddy. "Now he is fucking dead and the word is this Jamaican name Key-Tee is the one that pulled the trigger."

"Wait, did you say Jamaican Key-Tee?" Terrance asks Freddy, "Yes. That is the word," said Freddy.

"I know Key-Tee, Fred. He is a real murderers dude, a contract killer. There is no way this was random. This had to be a hit if Key-Tee did it."

Juan could see the wheels spinning in Freddy's head. There was much more to this story. Something was missing and Freddy needed to find out exactly what it was.

Four a.m. and Jackie heard her doorbell ringing. She thought that she was dreaming. There was no way someone would dare knock on her door this late. As she climbed out of bed, her phone started ringing "WTF?"

It was Kenny. She knew it was him because her caller ID read bad news. The doorbell ringing stopped and the loud knocking started next. Jackie looked out the peephole and there stood bad news, Mr. Kenny Thomas himself. She opens the door with an attitude, but before she could cuss Lucky Lefty out, he fell into her arms and started crying uncontrollably.

"What's wrong? What's wrong baby?" Jackie asked.

"They killed my best friend! My best friend is gone!" A sobbing Lucky Lefty said.

"Who?" ask Jackie.

"Jacob! They killed Quick Money!" said Lucky Lefty.

Jackie was speechless. She had never seen Kenny this vulnerable and she felt so bad for him. The fact that he was under investigation and could be jeopardizing her freedom did not matter at the time. Jackie just wanted to be there for him.

*   *   *

It was around five a.m. Lisa was laying in Terrance and Kay's guest room. Her hands were still shaking from the adrenaline running and pumping through her veins; it almost felt like a shot of pure MDMA. Lisa was also very worried and shook about her brother Pistol Pete's well-being. Doctor Peterson had already told the family that Pistol Pete's surgery went well, but it was really up to Pete if he was going to live through the night or not. All the signs were showing that Pete was still not out of the woods just yet. This was a nightmare scenario. Pistol Pete was still laying in the hospital bed shot the fuck up and fighting for his life. While she herself had just killed two people in an apartment building where any innocent bystander standing around looking could have witnessed the crime. Camp5 and the Down 4

Myne Crew were now at war and she still had four showcases to plan. Business was always first. No matter what! *What a hell of a day,* Lisa was thinking to herself.

Terrance always, I mean always, thought about everything before he made his next move. That was the only way he was taught to think by his OG's before him—stay focused, stay sharp. Terrance even took some of the baby gangster suggestions. Balance was everything to Tee, but right now without Pete, he wasn't feeling so balanced. Lying in bed, one of the things running through Terrance's mind was Pistol Pete. Terrance knew there was nothing that he could do at this point to save his partner Pete's life, but pray. There was only one thing to do that could halfway fix this problem and that was killing Lucky Lefty and the Down 4 Myne Crew, taking them all out for good. Throughout all of the chaos, Terrance had forgotten about his first showcase in two weeks in New York City. Terrance was thinking maybe he should just cancel it but he knew Lisa wouldn't go for it. She was always strictly business. Terrance was thinking so hard that his brain felt like it was about to explode. He reached in the drawer and grab a sleeping pill. Ten minutes later, Terrance was fast asleep.

Chapter 24

Lucky Lefty called Fox and the rest of the Down 4 Myne Crew to meet him at the spot. Lucky did not get any rest last night. Neither did Fox, Cory, or Travis. Everyone was in shock that Quick Money was dead. And no one really knew the answer to why, but Lucky Lefty. It was an awkward silence when Lucky Lefty walked downstairs to the basement. Cory and Travis were on social media reading all the Rest in Peace comments. Fox was smoking a blunt and staring into space. Quick Money was a hard target to kill, Fox was thinking to himself. This had to be a setup. That's the only way for someone to get close enough to kill Quick Money.

Lucky Lefty sat down at the round table. The first thing that came out of his mouth shocked everybody, "The Camp5 Crew killed Quick Money!"

"What?" Corey and Travis jump up from the table.

"Let's go get them now!" said Fox.

"We can't handle them toe to toe. We don't have enough firepower. I am putting a plan together now."

"How do you know for sure Lucky?" asked Fox.

"I just know. Give me a few days to put the plan in motion. Everyone stays on high alert. We are code red," said Lucky Lefty.

*   *   *

Back at the Sheriff's Office, Jackie Diaz was sitting at her office desk thinking about Kenny. He had come over in the middle of the night and broke down about what happened to Quick Money.

 She had never seen him break down like he did last night. Detective Jones and Detective Smith were in the briefing room with Captain Rogers, the U.S. Marshals and the homicide department. The DEA was also present. They knew it was going to take the whole department to stop this blood bath. For the first time, Terrance's name and picture was on the "Big Board" in the briefing room. This was a breakthrough itself for the DEA. They had been watching Tee for four and a half years and still didn't have any solid evidence. The first big step for them was having him on their "Crazy Wall". Pete, Jason, Adrian, Lisa and James were also on their wall. The DEA was in a surveillance van at the hospital taking pictures and video of everyone that was at the hospital. The briefing went on for five hours. The Down 4 Myne Crew and Camp5 were the topic of discussion. No matter how many resources he needed, Captain Rogers was willing to use them all to take down these dangerous crews.

   Detective Jones felt bad for Terrance. He knew that Tee was one of the biggest drug dealers in central Florida. But he was also cool, honest and a great guy... if that makes any sense to a law-abiding citizen. When the briefing was over, Jackie waited until Detective Jones came out and asked him to please come into her office. She knew Marshal Douglas was paying close attention to her body language, so she flirted with Detective Jones to piss Marshal Douglas off.

"How are you doing this morning Detective Jones?" asked Jackie.

"I am good, but I should be asking you that."

"The department had a really eventful night last night. Three bodies dropped, two people dead and one still clinging to his life, right?"

"Yes, it's been a long twenty-four hours. I have not had any rest since yesterday," said Detective Jones.

"Well, you should come by later. I think I can give you something to ease your tension," Jackie said looking at Detective Jones with her sexy brown eyes.

That sounded very tempting to Jones, but he declined her offer because there was too much going on at the office and plus, he needed to warn Terrance that he and his crew were finally on the authority's radar. Detective Jones said exactly what Jackie wanted to hear. She was only flirting with him to make Marshal Douglas jealous and her plan worked.

* * *

Several weeks had already passed. The streets were quiet, but the air was still thick with tension. The first three showcases were days away. Terrance felt guilty having to go on without Pistol Pete. He was still in the ICU fighting for his life. Terrance spent a lot of his time at Pistol Pete's bedside reading books and talking to him as he lay lifeless in a coma.

Everything was in place with the jewelry showcases. Lisa made sure of that. All Terrance really had to do was go to the airport and get on the plane. The rest of the crew were all on edge. There was too much heat on them. The alphabet boys were on their trail, the Muck Boyz was in town, plus they had beef with the Down 4 Myne Crew. By now everyone in the city knew how the police found Quick Money. Lucky Lefty's right-hand man, shot the fuck up in an apartment with some Spanish chick laying dead beside him. Everyone knew Lucky Lefty was going to respond with vengeance. It was just a matter of the time before it all went down.

On the way to the airport, Terrance was praying that Pistol Pete would be awake and smiling when he got back in town off his business trip. There was no way Terrance was going to propose to Kay without Pete being there to witness it. The Miami trip was supposed to be special. Everyone comes together to celebrate success, love, family and his retirement from the drug game. Instead, Terrance was on his way to New York without his best friend. This just didn't feel right to him. Lisa and James were already in New York putting everything together. The rest of the crew stayed behind to make sure that the business back home moved smoothly as usual.

Chapter 25

Lucky Lefty's mind was racing like the Daytona 500. Almost a month had gone by since he had lost his best friend Quick Money. The Down 4 Myne Crew was on edge. Everyone was waiting on the boss to give the kill order, but Lucky had to put together a solid plan not only to kill the Camp5 Crew, but to also take them out of business forever. The only loose ends were the Jamaican posse. Lucky needed their manpower for this plan to go off just right. The only problem, Key-Tee was already too hot, so Lucky knew that he couldn't use Key-Tee personally. This was going to have to come from an out-of-town crew that no one in town knew of. Lucky was waiting on the word to come from his brother Spider in prison. Lucky had sent a kite two weeks ago.

Lucky was wondering what could be taking Spider so long to get back at him. Patience was the last thing Lucky Lefty had at this point in time. Corey and Travis had been tailing a Spanish chick for the last two weeks, with no clue of why. All they knew was that Lucky Lefty asked them to stay close to her and report back to him on her every move. That was cool with Corey and Travis because Shawty was bad and all of her friends were also good looking. Lucky finally got the call he had been waiting on. "What's good Lil brother".

"I am in the box right now, sorry for the delay. That kite had to go through a few more channels than usual," said Spider. "Sorry to hear about Quick Money he was a solid foot soldier," Spider then continued on to ask Lucky Lefty, "So exactly what do you need from me baby brother?"

Lucky Lefty told Spider that he needed a clean-up crew from out of town that could get in and get out. Lucky also let his big brother Spider know the job was worth seven figures easy and everyone was guaranteed to walk away with six figures if the job went off without a hitch. The crazy part about this shit was that Spider raised Terrance and Lucky Lefty. They both came up under Spider's teachings. Things started to go west between Lucky and Terrance around Spider's seven-year stretch. After Lucky Lefty and Terrance split up, the underbosses and foot soldiers choose their sides, Camp5 or the Down 4 Myne Crew. Spider never got involved in their beef. He chose to always stay neutral. Terrance wasn't his blood brother, but to Spider blood meant nothing. Having loyalty was everything.

Terrance made sure Spider's life sentence was easy as he could possibly make it. Spider didn't have to worry about anything. His books were reloaded every month. Tee treated Spider like he was his big brother. That was another thing that made Lucky Lefty jealous. Even his own blood brother, loved this nigga Tee more then he loved him. Lucky knew he could never tell Spider that the crew he needed was for Terrance and the Camp5 Crew. Spider would never approve of it, but what Spider didn't know wouldn't hurt him.

Spider asked Lucky Lefty how Pistol Pete was doing. Even in lockdown he heard that someone had gunned down Pete at the strip club. Lucky played dumb and acted like he didn't have any information on Pistol Pete being shot. Lucky played like it was just a random shooting. Spider gave Lucky the information that he needed. Before Spider hung up the phone, he told his little brother to make peace with himself and to make peace with Terrance, "because hate is a terrible burden to carry."

Lucky Lefty told his big brother that he loved him and then Lucky hung up the phone. Everything was in place; it was finally time to make the move that he and Quick Money had been planning for the last nine months. The only difference was Quick Money wouldn't be here to see it through. Lucky knew his dawg was somewhere watching their plans play out. Tatiana and her two home girls were in the nail shop getting ready for a night out on the town with Adrian. With all that was going on everybody just needed to blow off a little steam, go out and have a few drinks.

Around eight-thirty p.m., Tatianna and her friends pulled into a bar called the Blue Haven Lounge. It was laid back and low key. The club's dress code was strict so that kept down a lot of confusion. A lot of them young guys didn't believe in the casual dress code, so the regular customers were mostly old heads and women with careers. Corey and Travis were parked off in the cut when they noticed Adrian standing outside talking to Tatiana and her friends. It all started to make sense then. Lucky Lefty knew these chicks would lead them straight to these Camp5 niggas. Corey and Travis couldn't believe how sharp and on point their boss Lucky Lefty was! Travis hurried up and called Lucky to let him know what the business was. Lucky Lefty told them to stay out of sight and keep a close tail on them. Adrian was inside mingling with Tatiana and her friends at the bar for about two hours.

Travis and Corey continued to wait outside until everyone came out and got into their cars. They followed them for the rest of the night. Finally, after around six hours of surveillance. Adrian and the girls were pulling up to the Bayside Apartments. Travis parked down the street and got out on foot to pursue Adrian and their entourage the rest of the way. Corey waited behind in the car to keep a lookout for any and everything that looked funny or out of place. Fifteen minutes later, Travis jumped back in the car and called Lucky Lefty. "Boss! I know what apartment they are chilling at." Lucky Lefty said "Bet" and hung up the phone!

Chapter 26

The New York showcase was beautiful. Lisa had every "T" crossed and every "I" dotted. The ballroom looked amazing. Everybody that was somebody on the New York scene was at this event. Everyone knew that Terrance and Lisa were great hosts from all the extravagant parties they used to have on New Year's Eve. The food was delicious, a thousand dollars a plate. Terrance made sure that he donated the proceeds to his charity, Save The- Inner-City Youth. Tee knew selling drugs was wrong, but if he could stop the younger kids from going down that dark path then he was all for it no matter how much of his time or money it took. James could tell that Terrance was off of his game, from the lack of emotion on his face. So, he took up a lot of Tee's slack with his guests. It was a lot going on back home, but the show had to still go on. No matter what the crew may have been facing back in Florida. The DEA had the building under surveillance, trying to blend in with the rest of the guests. Lisa noticed them standing out like a sore thumb. Detective Jones had already given Terrance the heads up, so Lisa made sure that the museum and the security were both airtight. Terrance's body was physically present but his mind was back in Florida with Pistol Pete. The night was finally coming to an end. The money bag was secure and all the customers were satisfied.

As soon as Lisa got back to her room, she emailed Tee and James their itinerary for the flight to LAX in the morning. Los Angeles was the second leg of the showcase. Terrance and Lisa both knew that Los Angeles was going to be more of a red-carpet event. The who's who, showing off the beautiful pieces provided by Exquisite House of Diamonds, Inc. while walking the red carpet for the "Busted" movie premier. Terrance's childhood friend Chucky James wrote and produced the movie *Busted*, so Tee was super excited to be there to witness his friends' success. It also was a great opportunity to show off his collection of jewelry while enjoying his partner's movie premier.

Los Angeles was like a breath of fresh air to Terrance, James and Lisa. It also was a major plus to Terrance that the medical marijuana was recreational in Los Angeles. Tee made sure to tell his Uber driver to stop by the dispensaries to grab an ounce of Pure Kush to help him with his insomnia because all he needed right now was a good night's sleep and a California king size bed to lay down in. James was also happy to be in Los Angeles. He had a few bad honeys out there that he hadn't seen in a while. For him, this was a perfect time to let off a little steam. Lisa was sneaky as hell, so no one really knew what she was up to. Lisa was the Camp5 Queen and she wore the title well with dignity, loyalty, love, and respect. She was Camp5's backbone. They all called her the Mother Earth of the family.

*   *   *

Back home in Florida, Freddy was getting very impatient while sitting in Clewiston waiting for Terrance to get back off his fancy trips. Freddy trusted Terrance and that was the only thing holding him back from making a move on Key-Tee and his pussy ass crew of Jamaicans. Freddy knew that Terrance had brains and that Terrance never moved off of emotion. The bigger picture was the only thing that Freddy had to go on right now. His second in charge Juan was ready to get it in, but he knew no one moved until Freddy gave the green light. Right now, the green light was on Terrance and Terrance was out of state handling business, so all of the gangster and murdering revenge shit was on hold for now. *"Just for now Freddy thought to himself."*

Lucky Lefty, the Feds and everyone else that was trying to take down the Camp5 Crew was moving in closer. Terrance could feel the walls closing in. The pressure was starting to build up, but Terrance and his crew were built for this. There was no way that they were about to be taken down without a fight.

The next morning came fast. Terrance was well rested from the Pure Kush he smoked the night before. He knew that they had the red-eye flight out of LAX. Terrance called up Lisa and James and invited them to brunch and some Beverly Hills shopping. Tee knew Lisa was always down for shopping and spending his money. They all met up down in the hotel lobby and caught an Uber truck to a restaurant on Wilshire Boulevard. After eating and plotting on the Atlanta trip, they pulled into the Beverly Center. Lisa was ready to hit the designer stores. She already knew exactly what she wanted. James and Terrance were ready to go to the Flight Club and grab some fresh new kicks, but they both knew to let Lisa do her shopping first or else it would be hell to pay. After a day of shopping, Terrance and James went back to the room to grab some drinks and finish smoking on that ounce of Kush that Terrance grabbed from the dispensary the night before. After they grabbed a snack to eat, they headed to Hollywood Hills to hang out with Chuck until it was time to fly out to Atlanta later that night. Lisa left Terrance and James after she got done blowing a bag at the designer stores. She called her own Uber and told Terrance that she had some business to handle and she would meet them at the LAX airport later. Terrance never questioned Lisa. He just told her to be safe and give him a call if she needed him for anything.

Lisa pulled up to a mansion in the Hidden Hills. When her driver pulled into the driveway there stood a beautiful Latina female dressed in an all-black sundress with some red bottom Christian Louboutin sandals on to match her sundress. Her face and body were flawless. She favored Khloe Kardashian with a body like the late 90s Jennifer Lopez. Everything was in place just like it was supposed to be. Lisa jumped out of the truck greeted the beautiful young lady with a kiss and proceeded to go inside. The house was amazing, with a view overlooking the beautiful valleys of California. Roberto was very happy to see his only niece, Lisa. She was his oldest brother's bastard child. Half Colombian and half black. The first nineteen years of her life, Roberto didn't even know that Lisa existed; she was from his brother's secret life in Florida.

Eight o'clock came around so fast that Terrance and James were almost late arriving at the airport. LA traffic was always hell to maneuver through around the rush hour. Lisa pulled up to the LAX airport in a Rolls Royce Ghost, black on black. Her uncle was a major player in Hollywood. He always asked Lisa to move out west with him, but she could not bear the thought of leaving Terrance and her Florida family and lifestyle behind that she had built for herself. James was the first to get onto Lisa about the car she had just jumped out of. He was the jokester of the crew, "damn baller I see you shining," said James.

Lisa just blew James' ass off with a "Boy please. Just get my bags out the trunk. We have a flight to catch."

Terrance knew about Lisa's powerful uncle, but he also knew how he felt about black people, especially the drug dealing kind. He never questioned her about that side of the family. It was always more of a need to know the basis for him. The one thing Terrance did know, is that Lisa had some fine ass Columbian cousin, back when Tee was still playing the games.

Terrance fell in love with one of Lisa's first cousins. Her name was Isabella Gomez. Terrance almost lost Kay behind Isabella. The two ladies even got into a fist fight at one of Terrance's condos on the coast of Tampa, Florida. That was a wild night. Terrance was shaking his head reminiscing thinking to himself. The crew boarded their red-eye flight headed to Atlanta for the third leg of their showcase. James was super excited about the Atlanta trip! "Strip club heaven." James had already called Adrian and Jason to meet them in Atlanta. This was about to be one hell of a weekend.

*   *   *

Back home, the authorities were preparing for the biggest sting operation ever in Highlands County history. Captain Rogers was rallying the troops, getting everyone in position to take down these two powerful drug-dealing crews that had been running his city streets for the past decade. Jackie was texting Lucky Lefty on her burner phone when U.S. Marshal Douglas walked in her office. "Did I scare you?" asked Marshal Douglas.

"No, you just surprised me a little, that's all. How can I help you?" Jackie responded.

"I was just wondering about Detective Jones. Something seems very off about him. Every time someone brings up Terrance Young's name in the briefing room, Jones always seems to go into defense mode," said Marshal Douglas. "I figured since you know the guys better than I do, maybe you could give me a little history lesson on their relationship?" asked Marshal Douglas.

Jackie's plan was working out perfectly. She already knew that Douglas was jealous of her and Detective Jones' relationship, and she also knew Douglas would go extra hard to prove that Detective Jones was the mold in the department. So, Jackie played Marshal Douglas' little cat and mouse game.

"The only thing I really know about the two of them is that they both grew up in the same neighborhood. I heard they were really close," said Jackie. Marshal Douglas' eyes lit up.

"Thanks for the intel, Ms. Diaz." He kissed Jackie on the cheek and rushed out of the room.

Chapter 27

Adrian and Jason were on the way to Orlando International Airport to catch a short forty-minute flight to Hartsfield-Jackson Atlanta Airport to meet up with the rest of the crew. On the way there, Adrian was telling Jason how he felt like someone was following him two nights ago when he was hanging out with Tatiana and her home girls at the Blue Haven Lounge. Jason told Adrian, "You already know our motto: total paranoia is total awareness. You can never be too safe out here, especially with everything we have going on right now." Adrian nodded his head in agreement with Jason because he knew that what Jason was saying was a hundred percent true.

*   *   *

Key-Tee called a meeting with Black Boy and his crew. The first topic of discussion was the Muck Boyz. He asked Black Boy when was the last time that he heard from them. Things had been really quiet ever since the night at the warehouse; something about this just really felt fishy to Key-Tee.

Black Boy explained to Key-Tee that he had not heard from Freddy or his goons in a few weeks. The last thing that he heard was that they were back down in Clewiston laying low after all the recent shootings. Key-Tee sent two hitters down south to check on the situation. This time around he was determined to take the pressure to the Muck Boyz in their own backyard!

Key-Tee had already moved over two thousand pounds of the weed for Adrian. Business was never better for him. No matter how much the police were cracking down, Key-Tee had his soldiers in the streets... hustling rain, sleet, hail or snow. There was plenty of money to be made for Key-Tee. Everyone else was scared to move except Key-Tee Jamaican posse. Key-Tee's turf was Key-Tee's turf and no one dared to step on Key-Tee's turf, no matter what city or what block! Key-Tee had a spot in Polk County, Desoto County, Highlands County, Okeechobee County and parts of Orlando and Tampa on lockdown. It was nothing for him to move five hundred pounds a week. That was light work for Key-Tee's crew. The Warlords made a name for themselves in America as one of the toughest crews out of Jamaica Queens, New York. Key-Tee killed his way to the top of the food chain. He was like a ghost. If Key-Tee wanted you dead, it was only a matter of time and you would be.

*   *   *

Lisa, James, and Terrance landed at the Atlanta Hartsfield-Jackson Airport around six-fifty a.m., everyone was well-rested. Los Angeles was relaxing and the overnight red-eye flight to Atlanta was very comfortable. It kind of felt like sleeping home on the Lazy Boy recliner. Terrance thought to himself. Jason and Adrian were already at the Camp5 Estate in

Alpharetta Georgia waiting for the rest of the crew to get there. The interior decorators and party planners were also there waiting for Lisa to arrive to give them instructions on the layout for the showcase. Terrance suggested that they have the showcase at the Alpharetta Estate because it was too hot to have it in the city of Atlanta with all the heat that was coming down on them from the Feds. James, Adrian, Jason and Terrance jumped in the SUV and headed downtown for some last-minute shopping and a little pleasure...well mostly pleasure. Atlanta was the capital for the strip club scene and there was no way James and Adrian were about to miss this opportunity of Chocolate Pleasure. Jason and Terrance's excuse was the wings and drink specials. James and Adrian knew better. Them niggas wanted to see some ass and tits too they were not fooling nobody!

After spending a couple of thousand a piece on the day shift entertainment, the guys took care of their tabs and headed back to the northside of Atlanta to get ready for the showcase. Of course, James set something up for later. A private party by the pool was just what the doctor ordered. James was thinking good thing the estate was on forty acres with two guest houses and three pools because Lisa was not with the thot shit and everyone in the crew knew that. The showcase started around eight p.m. The driveway and red-carpet entrances filled with *Atlanta Housewives, Married to Medicine*, and *Love and Hip-Hop* reality show stars. Entertainment lawyers, record label executives and some of the biggest Rap and R&B stars were also in attendance. Lisa King's black book was one of a kind. Everyone wanted to be a part of anything that she was doing. Lisa always had the best music, food and entertainment. Her events were a reflection of her. Beautiful, sexy, and bold ambiance. Everything had to be on point when Lisa put it together.

5:00 a.m.

Four hard knocks and Freddy's door flew open with voices screaming, "Sheriff's Office! Lay the fuck down and put your hands behind your head."

Freddy was caught off guard. If not, he would have never surrendered so easily. "Freddy James, you are under arrest for the murder of Wayne Brown." Freddy had no idea who the fuck they were talking about. Freddy had so many bodies under his belt that they could have been talking about anybody. The Clewiston Sheriff's Office rounded up the rest of Freddy's crew except for his right-hand man Juan. Juan was down in Miami South Beach with his family for the weekend. When Juan got the news, he went underground immediately.

Terrance's phone started ringing early. Detective Jones' number popped up on the caller ID.

"What's up Jones?"

"How is the ATL treating you?"

"The peach state is treating me great," said Terrance. "You should have been here with me."

"I wish," said Detective Jones. "But we have a shit storm going on down here. I am just calling to give you a heads up"

Terrance paused for a minute. The last thing he needed was more bad news. First Pistol Pete, the Feds and the beef with the Down 4 Myne Crew. Terrance's exit out of the game was going to be a little rockier than he had originally expected. But hey, it all came with the game and he understood that. After a brief pause, Detective Jones explained to Tee what was going on with Freddy and the Muck Boys. He warned Terrance to stay as far away from this situation as possible because the Feds were trying to connect the dots and bring everyone down that was connected to this case. Terrance wasn't worried about the murder case because he knew nothing of it but Freddy and his crew getting locked up put a monkey wrench in his plans. Hanging up the phone with Detective Jones, Tee immediately started planning his next move. Freddy being taken off his chess board by the authorities made things a little more complicated. The Muck Boys were a major part of Tee's plan which now needed to be revised.

Terrance heard a light knock on his bedroom door.

After he said come in, Lisa walked in with a soft pink Petites Christelle Gown draped over her strawberry milk like skin. Lisa was amazingly beautiful. It was so hard for Terrance to block out the fact that they were just best friends and he figured secretly Lisa was always madly in love with him. She was just waiting for him to leave Kay behind. They were like Bonnie and Clyde without the sex life. "What's wrong Terrance? It looks like your mind is all over the place. Is there anything I can help you with?" asked Lisa as she laid down beside Tee.

Terrance laughed and said, "Yeah get your sweet-smelling ass off of me. I am already having a morning erection," Terrance said jokingly.

"Boy please," said Lisa. "You wish that you could have this. Besides, I don't think you would know what to do with it."

"Is that what you think?" said Terrance.

"No Terrance, that's what I know," as Lisa pulled herself closer to Terrance and laid her head on his chest and asked him, "How are we going to exit this game clean?"

"That's what I've been planning for the last three months," responded Tee. "My goal has always been for us all to get out of the game clean and become legit, but some way the game just always pulls us back in." After a moment of silence, Terrance spoke and said, "Lisa, I have given you every tool you need to survive in this game, with or without me. So, no matter what happens to me, you will always be able to move forward and be successful."

"But Terrance...," before Lisa could get the rest out, Tee put his finger on Lisa's lips and kissed her.

Electricity shot through Lisa bones and tears raced down her face. Not knowing how to feel she just kissed Terrance back and held on to him for dear life. Lisa was a very strong woman, but in Terrance arms she felt vulnerable. With all that was going on in their lives, no one understood one another better than them two. Lisa stopped kissing Terrance and looked him directly in his eyes.

"No matter what happens I will always have your back. I love you so much Terrance."

Terrance rolled Lisa over and got on top of her. His phone rang. "Hello. What's up Kay?" Lisa got up and left the room.

Chapter 28

Adrian was wondering why Terrance and Lisa were so quiet on the flight back home. He would have thought everyone would be excited after the great news Tee got this morning from Kay. Pistol Pete was alive and well... not well but definitely alive.

Kay called Terrance early this morning and told him that Pete had woken up out of his coma in the middle of the night. Pistol Pete was not talking because he still had the tubes down his throat, but he was responding by blinking his eyes and moving his fingers. Lisa was lost in her thoughts thinking about what happened between her and Terrance just several hours ago. Lisa never loved anyone like she loved Tee but Lisa knew Terrance could never be hers because he belonged to Kay and that was the truth of it all.

Terrance's mind was racing so fast: Pistol Pete, Kay, Lisa, the Feds, Lucky Lefty and his crew. Back and forth it went as he broke down each scenario in his head and how each one would play out over and over again. James and Jason were knocked out cold. The after-party went on into the wee hours of the morning and they were dog tired. Adrian was still up going hard from the rolls he and a chick name Ms. Bananas had taken. She told Adrian her stage name was Bananas because her pussy was wet and slippery like a banana peel and would drive him bananas. After that remark Adrian was locked in with her the rest of the night. I guess he fell for the banana in the tailpipe! Tee was laughing in his mind thinking about it...

The flight back home was a short one. After forty minutes in the air, they were landing at the private airport in Sebring, Florida. Mr. Pat was waiting on Lisa with an armed security guard to escort them back to the storefront with all of the jewelry leftover from the showcases. Adrian, Jason, Terrance, and James caught an Uber to Florida Hospital to check on Pete. Adrian used this opportunity to ask Terrance what's up with Lisa. She seemed off on the flight. Tee hunched his shoulders and said, "I don't know, maybe she is exhausted from all the trips we took the last few days". That was a good enough explanation for Adrian, so he laid back in his seat and let it go.

When the crew walked into Pistol Pete's hospital room, they were surprised to see him sitting up talking to the doctors. Tonya, Kay and Jamal were by his bedside holding everything down with all smiles. When Kay saw Terrance walk into the room she jumped up and hugged him. Tee was happy to see that his best friend was still alive, breathing and also talking. At that moment, Tee realized that all of his prayers had been answered. With so much pain in Pistol Pete's voice, he looked over at Terrance and said "What's up brother from another mother? Did you miss me?"

"Hell yeah!" Terrance replied and everyone in the room burst out laughing and said "Aww". In that single moment, everything felt back to normal. For several hours the crew sat around in Pistol Pete's hospital room laughing, joking and reminiscing about the old times. Pistol Pete asked Terrance where Lisa was hiding. Tee told Pete she went to drop the jewelry off and after that she went home to get some rest because she was very tired from the three showcases. "But she said to give you her love and she would be here bright and early tomorrow to check on you," Terrance told Pistol Pete.

"Everything went off without a hitch", said Jason. Gold sold money folds. Before anyone could go any deeper into the conversation, the nurse walked in and said visiting hours were over. Pistol Pete told Tonya to go home and check on their kids and give them a kiss for him. He knew she needed to get some proper rest. Tonya had barely slept in her own bed the last few weeks.

Before Terrance could leave the room, Pete asked him to stay for a second. Tee knew what it was about. Pete wanted to tell him details about the shooting at the strip club, Terrance thought. When Pete started talking, he shocked Terrance with what he had to say. Pistol Pete told Tee that he was right by wanting to get out the game. The code of the streets was the same but the people living by them had changed. It was time for them to find something else to do other than living the street life. "I heard that nigga Quick

Money no longer breathing. Him and the chick Rosalina had a rough night the day I got shot?" said Pistol Pete.

"Yeah," Tee responded. "You can thank Butterfly for that." Butterfly was Lisa's code name between the three of them.

"Oh word," said Pistol Pete.

Terrance bumped Pete up and walked out the room. "See you tomorrow pimp. Sleep tight..."

*　　　*　　　*

Lisa was laying on the couch watching TV trying not to think about what had happened earlier that morning between her and Terrance... She never let her emotions get the best of her especially when it came to her true feelings about Terrance Young. Lisa knew she had violated Kay's trust, but she also knew how much she really cared for Terrance. Hell, Tee practically raised her and Kay. In a perfect world they would all just live together as sister wives and get married, Lisa was thinking to herself. This was Lisa's first night staying home since the incident with Rosalina and Quick Money. Lisa had no choice because she didn't feel right staying at Terrance and Kay's house until everything was out on the table between her and Tee.

Kay was talking the entire way home but Terrance didn't really hear one word that she was saying. His mind was directly on Lisa. Tee knew Lisa loved him, but the emotions that she showed this morning was something totally different. The emotion that Tee showed Lisa was also something totally different. "That moment," "that kiss," "that second" they both realized that it was far too late and that the cards had been dealt. Everything was on the table. The damage had already been done.

"TERRANCE!"

"Huh? Oh, what was that you asked me bae?"

Kay immediately got pissed off. "What the fuck is on your mind that you are blatantly ignoring me?"

"A lot," Terrance answered. "I just need to get home and get some rest."

"Yeah, you do that," said Kay. The rest of the ride was in silence which is just what Tee needed.

*   *   *

Bright and early Lisa walked through Pistol Pete hospital room with flowers and a bottle of champagne. Lisa knew that the champagne would get Pete's blood boiling because Pistol was a straight Hennessy drinker. Pete jumped straight down Lisa's throat about the champagne. She immediately started laughing and told Pistol Pete that they were celebrating the fact that he was still alive and well.

Pete told Lisa, "Sis I would rather be dead than to drink that nasty ass shit." They both started laughing.

"So how are you really doing?" Lisa asked.

"Just happy to be still here. Terrance told me what you did for me. I owe you one sis," Pistol told Lisa with a very stern and sincere tone.

"Don't worry about it bruh. That's what family is for, we take care of one another no matter what! We ride together! We die together."

"So how was Cali, New York, and Atlanta?" Pete asked Lisa.

"A lot of work but we made a lot of money. It was well worth the grind," Lisa told Pete. "I saw my uncle and little cousin out in Cali. She asked me how you were doing."

"Oh, that's what's up," Pistol Pete smiled. Lisa's little cousin always had a crush on him but Pete knew her uncle was crazy and didn't like black people. He could only imagine what he would do to one that was dating his daughter. "What's on your mind sis?" Pistol Pete asked Lisa.

Lisa started crying and told Pistol Pete she fucked up in Atlanta. After thirty minutes of pouring out her heart to him about Terrance and Kay, Pistol Pete set up in his hospital bed in silence for a minute or two. Then replied, "Well Sis. I know Kay's is going to be pissed off, but you can't help how you feel. Have you told Terrance any of this yet?" Pistol Pete asked.

Lisa said, "No. I just got off the plane, went to the storefront, dropped the jewelry off, went straight home and cried myself to sleep."

Pistol Pete was shocked because Lisa never cried. She was tougher than nails. This thing with her and Terrance was way more serious than he initially thought it was. Pistol Pete felt like he was stuck in the middle because Kay was his blood sister and Lisa was just like his blood sister. All Pistol Pete could think about was, *damn. What has my brother Terrance got himself into this time with these two alpha female dragons?*

"I will die for that man. Anything he asks me, I will give to him without ever asking him why," Lisa said with such a serious look on her face. Before Pistol Pete could reply, Kay, Terrance, and Tonya walked into the hospital room.

Chapter 29

Lucky Lefty was running some last-minute drop-offs before he was set to meet up with the cleanup crew that Spider plugged him in with. Lucky Lefty had been watching the Camp5 Crew's every move. Week in and week out ever since Quick Money and Rosalina got killed... Lucky knew about the showcases out of state and he also knew that Pistol Pete had survived Quick Money's attempt to murder him which made Lucky Lefty's blood boil knowing that his brother died for nothing.

Lucky laid in bed many nights tempted to pull up to the Florida Hospital dressed like a doctor and just finish the job that his brother Quick Money had started. Plotting his revenge was so sweet but taking down Terrance and that bitch Lisa was something a little more than revenge. That shit was personal for Lucky Lefty... Lucky pulled up to the trap house to meet up with the Down 4 Myne Crew to go over all the plans before he met up with the cleaning crew later on that night. Corey, Travis and Fox were all ready to take orders from their general. The wait had been way too long and everyone was ready for payback.

* * *

Meanwhile... U.S. Marshall Douglas had plans of his own. Douglas was busy building a case against Terrance, Kenny and both of their crews. He also was secretly investigating Detective Jones and the rest of

Highlands County Sheriff's Office. Tommy Douglas knew this case ran much deeper than the surface and he intended on getting to the bottom of it. The more Marshal Douglas searched; the more things got complicated.

What Douglas couldn't understand was how Kenny Thomas, aka Lucky Lefty, had survived so long without being busted. Him and his crew were very messy. Terrance on the other hand, he could understand. The guy was clean as a whistle. Nothing pointed to Tee being dirty. It was going to be hard to convict him of any crime, Marshal Douglas thought to himself.

*   *   *

Lucky left the trap to meet up with Jose, his brother Spider's outside connection. After an hour-long meeting, everything was put into play. Camp5 was finally about to get what they deserved and Lucky Lefty was happy to be the one to deliver the package.

What Lucky Lefty didn't know is that Slim got out to set him and Fox up on a murder that they committed when they were teenagers. The two of them were coming back from Tampa, Florida with two kilos of heroin in the car and got stopped by a state trooper. Fox didn't even know what was going on until he heard two shots and watched the trooper's lifeless body drop to the ground. Lucky pulled off from the scene, got rid of the gun, dope, and the car. A cold case of that magnitude being solved would definitely give Spider his freedom.

Spider knew why his little brother wanted a crew. He also knew he and Terrance were in a major beef. He also knew his little brother would reach out to him for the help he needed to take Terrance out. The only thing Spider cared about was his freedom and his dumb ass brother killing Slim took any chances of that ever happening off the table. Terrance went to visit Spider out of respect that he was Lucky Lefty's older brother and also his OG. Terrance needed the green light to kill Lucky and after an hour and a half visit, Spider gave him the ok to take his little brother out. The plan was in motion and everything was in place. Lucky and the Down 4 Myne Crew were finally about to be a distant memory.

Chapter 30

Kay was in the kitchen cooking when she heard the doorbell ring. Strange... because she knew she hadn't buzzed anyone in the gate.

Lisa was standing at Kay and Terrance's front door ringing the doorbell, so nervous that she forgot that she had her own key to the house.

Kay opened the door. "Girl, why don't you just use your key?" Kay asked Lisa.

Lisa really didn't have an answer. She was trying to figure out the same thing. For some reason she had not been herself ever since the Atlanta trip. Kay asked Lisa to come into the kitchen and help her finish the feast that she was cooking for the family tonight. Pistol Pete was out of the hospital and everyone was coming over to Kay and Terrance's house for family dinner and a welcome home party.

Kay was going on about how happy she was about Pete's recovery going so well and how blessed they all were to have one another. Kay could feel that something was wrong with Lisa, because the look on Lisa's face told it all. "What's wrong Lisa?" Kay asked.

Lisa looked at Kay with tears in her eyes and said, "Sorry sis, but I am in love with Terrance..."

*   *   *

Terrance and Pistol Pete were on their way to the honeycomb hideout to meet up with the rest of the crew and to talk business with them about their final attempt to get out of this game for good. When they entered the house, everything was dark except downstairs. Pistol Pete and Tee pulled out their handguns... shit felt really shaky.

Pete wasn't into getting shot again. That shit was out of the question for him. As they walked down the stairs, they saw Adrian, James, Jason and Jamal standing over two people tied down and bound to chairs with blindfolds on. Terrance asked Jamal what the fuck was going on. Before he could answer, Adrian said, "I caught these two imposters following me. So, I baited them in and called for the rest of the guys to ambush them."

Pistol Pete said, "So what do we have here?" With a smirk on his face as he lifted the blindfolds off Corey and Travis' head. Immediately Travis started cursing and talking shit to the whole crew. He actually spit at Terrance and told Pistol Pete that he was a dead man walking. Without hesitation, Pistol Pete put one in his head and four in his chest.

Corey was shaking with fear in his eyes as Pete turned the gun on him and calmly asked him, "Now how do you want to do this?" Corey burst out crying, "I will tell y'all anything you want to know! Just don't kill me!"

Terrance told Corey, "Too late. I already know everything. Don't worry, your boss Lucky will be visiting you in hell real soon," and knock Corey brains everywhere with his 40 Caliber. "Get somebody here to clean this shit up James, we have business to discuss," said Terrance.

*   *   *

Marshal Douglas had everything he needed to get his conviction on Kenny, aka Lucky Lefty. He just had to convince the District Attorney that Detective Jones was the leak and this would be an open and shut case. Meanwhile, Detectives Smith and Jones had a three o'clock meeting with a witness that said that they had some information on the apartment double homicide that involved the Spanish woman and Quick Money. This was the first real breakthrough that the department had gotten since the event took place a few weeks back. What Detective Jones heard was disturbing. The witness described a pretty female that looked like she could be mixed leaving the apartment after the shots rang out. She said that she was afraid, so she went back inside her apartment and locked her doors. Detective Smith asked her what was the reason that she was coming forward with information now. She said because she wanted justice for the victims and she thought no one deserved to die like that, she went on explaining to the two detectives. Jones already had an idea of who the suspect was but he wasn't saying anything about this to his partner Detective Smith.

*   *   *

Lucky Lefty and Fox were sitting at the trap house waiting on Travis and Corey to pull up. They had a lot to do today and these niggas were already an hour and half late and neither one of them were answering the phone. Lucky told Fox, "Let's go, we have to meet up with the team my brother Spider put together for us to take out Terrance and his crew. We will get up with them fools later". Fox told Lucky, "You are a smart guy for not telling Spider what the crew he put together was really for because he would have never gone for it if he knew what we were really up to. Spider has a soft spot for Terrance," Fox went on saying to Lucky Lefty on the way out the door.

Lucky and Fox pulled up to the meeting spot and jumped out. When they walked in the building, Marshal Douglas and two other undercover Narcotic Officials were looking like straight goons, killers and hitmen.

"Are you ready to do this?"

Lucky responded, "You know I am. What's the plan?"

Chapter 31

Detective Jones pulled up to meet up with Terrance. He told Terrance it was urgent and could not be discussed over the phone.

"We have a major problem on our hands. That double homicide involving that Spanish chick and Quick Money, a witness has come forward and she is describing a suspect that looks just like Lisa. Now I have not said anything to my partner about all of this, but it won't be long until he figures this thing out and puts two and two together. You need to get Lisa out of the states before she becomes a person of interest. The DEA is waiting for a reason to take you down and this would be a perfect opportunity for them to do it."

Terrance listened to everything Detective Jones was saying. At the same time, he was devising a plan in his mind. There was no way he was about to let Lisa take the fall for this.

"This is the last time I can reach out to you without incriminating myself in this investigation. You are on your own now. I wish you well and safe travels my friend," Detective Jones told Terrance as he got in his unmarked sedan.

Terrance jumped back in his car and shut the door. Pistol Pete was sitting there waiting impatiently. "What did he have to say?" Pistol Pete asked Terrance.

"Pete, I think Lisa is about to get indicted for Rosalina and Quick Money's murder. Jones said they have a witness that came forward today and she heard everything. She also may be able to point her out in a line up."

"Well Tee, that only means one thing." Terrance knew what Pete was saying, but he also knew it had to be another way.

Back at the house, Lisa had just broken the big news to Kay. As soon as the words left Lisa's mouth, Kay slapped the shit out of Lisa. Under normal conditions, Lisa would have never allowed this but she knew that she was in the wrong and had really betrayed her friend's trust. "I am so sorry Kay! I am so sorry, I never meant to hurt you!" Lisa cried out.

"How long has this betrayal been going on?" Kay asked Lisa. "How long have you been fucking my man? You high yellow bitch! How long?!"

"We never had sex! I promise you sister! We never took it that far. We only—" Before Lisa could get it out, Kay slapped Lisa again. This time Lisa was coming towards Kay about to light her ass up. As soon as Lisa drew back to punch Kay, Terrance jumped in front of her.

"I knew you were fucking that high yellow bitch the whole damn time Terrance! How could you do this to me?" Kay was yelling at the top of her voice.

Terrance was confused because he and Lisa only shared a kiss and that was it. Before Tee could get anything out, Kay told Terrance, "You don't have to ever worry about seeing your unborn child. We will no longer be a part of your life. Go be with that bitch and sell drugs for the rest of life."

Terrance was shocked that Kay said anything about him selling drugs and Lisa was even more shocked to know that Kay was pregnant. Kay wasn't dumb. She knew Tee still was messing around with the game, she just ignored it because she had seen so much of a great change in him. Lisa was standing there in disbelief. She pushed Terrance's hands off her and said, "I got to get out of here."

"Wait Lisa!" said Terrance.

"That's right bitch! Get the fuck out of my house!" Kay was yelling over her brother Pistol Pete's shoulders while pointing a knife at the same time.

Terrance followed Lisa out the door. "Wait Lisa! Wait! It's something you need to know..."

"I just found out everything I needed to know," Lisa responded to Terrance. "Do you know how much I love you Tee? Do you? No, you can't because if you did you would have told me Kay was pregnant. You are sad Terrance, just sad." Lisa jumped in her Bentley coupe and sped off.

As Terrance walked back in the front door Kay started going off again.

"Why are you coming back in here?" Kay asked Tee. "No good ass nigga! Get your shit and leave now! I never want to see you again!"

Pistol Pete was trying to calm his sister down. She looked at Pete and told him to also get the fuck out her house. Kay was in a rage and no one could calm her down. The dogs were barking and disturbed by all of the commotion that was going on inside the house.

Terrance and Pete jumped in the car and left the house. Pete called Tonya and gave her a small version of what was going on and told her to go and check on Kay. Tonya was steaming hot. She called her brother trifling and said all three of them belong together, referring to Lisa, Terrance and Pete.

"Damn Terrance, what are you going to do about this situation?" Terrance heard Pete, but he couldn't respond. His mind was blank, still trying to figure out what the hell just happened. How did he lose his best friend and the love of his life in a matter of minutes and how was he going to fix this?

Chapter 32

Adrian was on the phone with Key-tee about another shipment of high-grade marijuana coming in. Key-tee was moving them faster than Adrian could give them to him. It was amazing how the supply had disappeared so fast with the heat that was coming down. Adrian and Jamal were going to miss Key-tee's business. That Jamaican was a hustling ass dude.

The meeting was set up for seven-thirty p.m. Jamal called Terrance and told him everything was a go and everyone was in place.

*   *   *

Meanwhile back at the Sheriff's Office, Jackie was working her magic and covering up her tracks to make sure her name was in the clear. No one would ever expect her to leak information to Lucky Lefty and his crew after all of the groundwork she had laid to pin it all on Detective Jones. The day had finally come. Captain Rogers' teams had put everything in play. Everyone was on their job... SWAT, DEA, US Marshals and the local authorities. Captain Rogers called one last early morning briefing to make sure everything and everyone was in place and ready to go.

The tension in the briefing room was intense and the air was thick. Everyone could tell something was going on between US Marshal Douglas and Detective Jones, but the most important thing was making sure no one from either crew escaped the long arm of the law. Captain Rogers gave everyone their assignments. The plan was set. Before Lucky Lefty and his crew were supposed to take out Terrance and the Camp5 Crew, the authorities were to rush in and take everyone down without anyone getting hurt. They had enough evidence on Kenny Thomas, aka Lucky Lefty, to put him away forever. The DEA was still building their case on Terrance and his crew, but they still had enough evidence to charge him and Lisa with conspiracy to commit two counts of first-degree murder. The pictures that they took outside the hospital of him and Lisa walking and talking the night Pistol Pete got shot were just a fraction of the evidence they were building on him and Lisa.

Everything was set and the meeting was over. On the way out of the briefing room, Douglas bumped into Jones and whispered, "I know what you've been up to, you dirty pig."

Jones shoved Douglas and started yelling, "If you got a problem with me, we can handle it you little bitch!"

The other officers got in between the two of them. That's when Detective Jones told Marshal Douglas, "Yea I am sleeping with Diaz. Is that why you mad huh? I will tell her you said Hi tonight while I am celebrating with her little sweet Spanish pussy."

Marshal Douglas started smirking and said, "The only thing you will be enjoying tonight is sharing a jail cell with your partner Kenny Thomas."

Detective Smith and Detective Jones were looking so confused. What in the hell was this fool talking about? Jones hated Kenny Thomas and everyone in the department knew it. Marshal Douglas could see the look on all the other officers' faces after he made that last statement. Something was wrong. He had been played by Jackie and he knew it.

*   *   *

Tee pulled up to Lisa's condo. Terrance needed his plan to work in order to get everyone out of the state safely. Terrance came in through Lisa's garage door. She just laid there on the couch. "Listen baby girl, I know you are hurt and pissed off at me, but we gotta get you out of here. The Feds are coming and they have a witness that can place you at the scene of Rosalina's house that night of the murders."

Lisa sat straight up. This was one of her worst fears. That some nosy ass neighbors had spotted her coming out of Rosalina's apartment. "Fuck Tee my life is getting worse by the hour," Lisa told Terrance.

"No baby girl. What did I always tell you? No matter what I will always make sure you don't do one day in jail. I have an escape plan. Get everything that's important and meet me at this address in four hours." As Terrance turned around to walk out the condo, Lisa grabbed Tee's hand. Pulled him to her and started kissing him.

"I love you baby. Please don't be late," Lisa told Terrance. Terrance looked at Lisa right in her beautiful eyes. This was the first time he realized that he could not live without her.

Terrance said, "I love you too baby. I will be there waiting for you." Lisa was crying as Terrance was leaving out of the garage door.

"Be safe bae."

"I will," Terrance replied as the door closed behind him.

Over at Kay and Terrance's house, things were going much different for Pistol Pete. Kay was still mad and ready to fight everybody about the incident earlier but when Pete explained to her what was going on, she calmed down and immediately became concerned with her future child's father. "Listen Sis. get everything that's important and meet us at this address in four hours. We all have to disappear for a little while," Pete told Kay.

"I hope that bitch Lisa got her own route because she can't leave with us," Kay told her brother Pistol Pete.

"We don't have time for that Kay. Just get there on time. I am about to go and drop these damn dogs off at Jason's house. I will meet you there. Just don't be late," said Pistol Pete.

"I won't nigga! Damn! "Kay yelled at her brother.

*   *   *

Jason, Adrian and James were all in the clear for now. Neither one of them were on the radar. Once everything cooled off, they all had instructions to keep all the businesses running smoothly. Camp5's legal businesses were so air-tight, Terrance knew it was no way the federal government could touch any of it. Everyone knew what to do. If something ever happened like this, the crew was prepared for the worst-case scenario. No one was in panic mode.

Lisa's driver pulled up to the address that Terrance gave her. It was a private airport. Waiting on her was a fifteen-passenger jet. Lisa's driver grabbed her bags and she grabbed her own briefcase and her carry-on bags. As Lisa was walking up the jet staircase texting Terrance, Kay was staring out the window with nothing but hate in her eyes. Lisa felt someone staring at her. When she finally got onto the jet, she heard Kay's voice, "What are you doing here sour bitch?"

Lisa told Kay, "Look I don't have time for this. I told you I didn't fuck your man, but I am madly in love with him. Right now, we have more important matters on the table."

Kay didn't want to agree, but she knew Lisa was right so she just sat down in her seat and started texting Terrance.

Chapter 33

Key-tee called Lucky Lefty up and asked him to meet him at his warehouse to talk business about a new plug. Lucky Lefty knew he needed a new plug because they were about to be swimming in money once they got rid of Terrance and his crew. This was the perfect opportunity to expand and start looking to really get control of the streets. Fox was riding along with Lucky now because Quick Money was gone and Lucky Lefty just didn't trust anyone else to go anywhere with him at this point.

Lucky's phone rang as they were exiting off of the highway. It was Jose a.k.a. Marshal Douglas making sure everything was still on point for the massacre they had planned for Terrance and his crew. Lucky Lefty gave Douglas and his goons the exact instructions—kill everybody but Terrance. Lucky wanted to kill Terrance himself; no one was going to take that away from him.

*   *   *

Terrance made one last stop to his jewelry shop. He went in through his back office and took a black bag of money out of his safe. Tee locked the building back up, jumped in his car and hit the gas.

*   *   *

Jackie was just about to leave her office when Marshal Douglas walked in and slammed the door behind himself. "What the fuck is going on Diaz? Why did you lie to me about Detective Jones? What are you hiding WOMAN?" Douglas spoke with anger in his voice.

"What do you mean? I am not hiding anything," Jackie told Douglas.

"If I find out that you are lying to me, I am going to put you in a cell right next to your boyfriend. Are we clear?" Marshal Douglas slammed Jackie's door as he exited the room. At this point things were starting to get out of hand, Jackie was feeling the pressure and there was no way she was going down for Lucky Lefty and his group of thugs. She immediately went to her back up plan.

*   *   *

On the way over to Jamaican Key-tee's warehouse, Fox told Lucky he still hadn't heard from Corey and Travis. He was worried and really felt like something was wrong. Lucky felt the same way but he knew he had business to handle with Key-tee. When they pulled into the driveway of the warehouse, nothing looked out of place. The only vehicle there was Jamaican Key-tee's, so Lucky and Fox both put their guards down as they were entering the building.

Key-tee was sitting at the table in his office when Lucky and Fox entered. "What's up Lucky? I got a nice deal for you on the table. Have a seat and let's talk."

Lucky sat down. Fox stayed standing up, really looking and feeling uneasy. "So, what's this business you have for me that's so urgent and can't wait?" Lucky Lefty asked the Jamaican Key-tee.

"I am the urgent business," said Terrance as he walked out of the shadows. Before Fox could reach for his piece, Pistol Pete already had his 40 to the back of Fox's head.

"Don't you do it pussyfoot," Pistol Pete told Fox.

Lucky jumped up from the table, pulled his gun out and pointed at Terrance. "Tell me what's stopping me from killing you right now." Lefty asked Terrance.

Chapter 34

Detective Smith got an anonymous phone call that Jamaican Key-tee killed his confidential informant Slim for Kenny Thomas and they were about to meet at a warehouse. The anonymous caller also told them that they believe Jackie Diaz was the one leaking all of the information to Kenny Thomas. They also said that the two of them had a secret relationship going on. Detective Smith and Detective Jones rushed over to Key-tee's warehouse on Highway 64. Jones couldn't believe that he let this trifling bitch Jackie play him like a damn fool.

*   *   *

Meanwhile Jackie was headed home to grab her bags. She knew it was time to skip town. She could feel the walls crumbling down around her and she wasn't about to wait around to be crushed by them. Marshal Douglas was at the meeting spot getting prepared to meet up with Lucky Lefty and Fox to take out Terrance and his crew. Everyone was prepared for this successful exchange. All the agencies were in place. The details were simple. Let no one escape. Everyone involved was going down tonight.

*   *   *

Jason and James dropped off a bag for Terrance at the jet as they were told and disappeared without saying anything to Kay or Lisa. They both knew Terrance was a master thinker, so they didn't question anything that was going on. They both were nervous and kept looking out of the windows for Tee to pull up. They needed each other comfort, but neither wanted to admit it, so they both just sat there glued to their phones.

*   *   *

Detective Jones and Smith were a couple of minutes away from Key-tee's location. They would have called in for backup but the rest of the team was sitting on the spot where the massacre was supposed to go down. This was something they were going to have to handle on their own.

"So how do you want to play this?" Lucky Lefty asked Terrance.

"Tell your partner to put down his gun."

"Or what?" Terrance asked Lucky Lefty.

"What do you mean or what? I've been itching to kill you since we were kids. You always thought you were better than everybody else. Now what do you have to say before I take your life?"

"You know how I feel, Kenny. Every action has a reaction. Say goodnight"

"I can't let you do that, King." Key-tee unloaded the clip-on Lucky Lefty, before he could attempt to get off a shot at Terrance.

Pistol Pete blew Fox shit all over the table. Brains were everywhere. Jones and Smith heard the shots and started ducking back behind their squad car, calling for backup.

Terrance threw the bag of money on the table to Key-tee. "It's all there, five million. Do you need to count it?"

Key-tee was standing across the table looking at Tee with amazement. "Terrance you a cold ass Yankee boy, my youth. It was great doing business with you. Maybe again in the future?"

Terrance started to walk out of the warehouse and then suddenly turned around to Key-tee and said, "Yo King! I forgot something. You have a phone call," and threw Key-tee a burner phone. "It was on speakerphone."

"Yo who is this?" Key-tee asked.

"It's death knocking at your front door pussy ass Jamaican. This for my cousin Slim. Tell him I said his big cousin Freddy always got his back. Muck-boys for life... Juan, you know what to do."

Shots rang out and Key-tee's lifeless body dropped on the table. Juan spoke some words in Spanish and grabbed the bag with the five million and they all left out the back door.

Chapter 35

As Juan, Terrance and Pistol Pete were leaving the warehouse, Detective Jones and Smith were entering the warehouse. Detective Jones witnessed Key-tee, Fox and Lucky Lefty's lifeless bodies lying in a puddle of their own blood. All shot multiple times. All deceased. Detective Smith heard cars cranking up out back and ran for the back door. By the time he could get back there, he witnessed three cars fleeing the crime scene.

Listening over his radio, Marshal Douglas heard the commotions and flipped over the table. The only chance he had of solving this case was called in as a DOA. Kenny Thomas had gone and got himself killed. He knew Terrance had something to do with it, but he just couldn't put his finger on it.

An hour later... The Feds had Terrance house surrounded and they were questioning Kay's parents. Kay's mom said that she heard her son and daughter arguing and saying something about catching an airplane somewhere and then they rushed out together. DEA agents reached out to US Marshal Douglas and told them to lock all the airports in the area down because that's how Terrance and Lisa were getting out! Marshal Douglas' agents comb through all the major airports. There was no sign of Terrance, Lisa, nor Kay. They had to be flying out private, Douglas thought to himself.

Terrance and Pistol Pete were at the honeycomb hideout with the rest of the team going over all of the final details. Tee was leaving Pete in command until some of the heat was gone and he could figure everything out. Everyone was on point. Tee said his good-byes and headed out to the clear port. A lot of things were running through Terrance's head as he replayed the last six months back, but none of it compared to what he was facing on that airplane with Lisa and Kay.

Terrance pulled up to the airport. Kay and Lisa both started smiling with joy. The love of their lives had finally made it to them. Never mind what they were going through, they could handle that later. As Lisa and Kay were walking to the jet door to greet Terrance, police lights came out of nowhere and they were everywhere.

Lisa grabbed Kay, pulled her back inside and told the pilot, "We have to go now!" Kay was crying out of control as the jet doors lifted up. Terrance was surrounded by agencies all with their guns drawn on him. Tee was looking right through them. All he was concerned about at the time was making sure that jet took off.

Marshal Douglas looked at Terrance and said, "We got you now," and cuffed him.

Kay was weeping uncontrollably. Lisa looked at her and said, "Don't worry baby girl. I gotcha!"

TO BE CONTINUED...